SECRETS?

A Swedish Crime Novella

Stockholm Sleuth Series

CHRISTER THOLIN

Translated by Doreen Zeitvogel

Title of the original German edition:
GEHEIMNISSE?
Published 2017

Cover design by Rob Williams

ISBN of the pocketbook:
ISBN: 1549586645
ISBN-13: 978-1549586644

For my daughter, Anabel

Contents

1

The train rumbled into the underground station. Elin watched the platform, searching for the sign with the name of the stop: *Rådhuset*. So she had already made it to *Kungsholmen*, one of Stockholm's central islands and where she lived. Just two more stops before she would have to get off, and from there it was barely ten minutes to her apartment. Another workweek ended, and as was so often the case, a pretty dull one at that. She hadn't had much to do. Tobias, her boss, was out of the office most of the time, and she had had to sit at her desk and answer the phone. This was not at all what she had imagined.

For two years now, Elin had been working for a company called Secure Assist. She had only taken the job because in the beginning Tobias had promised her that, little by little, he would groom her to work in the field as a private investigator. Except that Tobias hadn't yet asked her a single time, let alone given her an assignment. Luckily, Lars, one of the private detectives, had asked for her twice in the past year. Those had been amazing assignments, and they had given her a chance to prove herself. She had even solved the second case almost entirely by herself. Yes, to some extent she had forged ahead without authorization, but she knew exactly what would happen if she asked permission for every move. Someone else would get the assignment, or they would tell her it was all too risky. Still, her heart was set on this job: her great dream in life was to be a good detective. And her education was the perfect fit. She had graduated with an IT degree, and she was also an outstanding close-combat fighter. Add to that her intuition and exceptional creativity when it came to finding out information. But Tobias liked to bet on more conventional careers, in other words, people who had formerly worked as bodyguards or security personnel—or, even better, for the customs office or, like Lars, the police. Elin's build may also have been an issue: she was small and slight, while Lars was close to 6'2", with broad shoulders. Unfortunately, there was nothing Elin could do about that, so she tried to use forceful behavior to make up for her lack of stature. Then again, being small could sometimes be an asset—like when you needed to hide.

Two young men shoved past her to get to the two empty window seats in Elin's section. Otherwise, the train was packed. And no wonder—it was rush hour on a Friday afternoon. Elin watched them. One was wearing earphones, with the cables tucked into his jacket pocket, and he was tapping his foot in time to the music that only he could hear. The other was holding a smartphone to his ear and talking about some newfangled program he absolutely had to buy. The train sped along as Elin's thoughts returned to her problem. She was determined to get another assignment, preferably with Lars. Lars owed her, anyway. She'd already saved his ass twice: the first time, as he lay unconscious on the ground after an explosion and she'd hauled him out of the fire danger zone; and the second time, when two child abductors were threatening him with a rifle. Both operations had happened at the end of the previous year. Now it was almost summer, and since then she'd done nothing but sit in the office and, other than secretarial work, procured some information now and then. That left her seriously frustrated. Nothing had helped—not talks with Tobias or pleading with Lars. The answer was always the same: there were no suitable assignments. True, most of the jobs consisted of boring sentry duties or humdrum surveillances, but Elin would have preferred even those to the office.

Finally, Elin set herself a deadline: if her job showed no basic change for the better by the end of the year, she would hand in her notice. She had already started to implement a parallel plan and had registered her own company. In Sweden, that was easy to do, and within one hour she had filled out all the online forms and digitally signed and submitted them. Just a week later, her company was official. She had chosen the simplest form of business: everything was in her name and, aside from a small registration fee, had cost nothing since there was no need to contribute your own capital. So now she had her own company that covered all the functions of a private detective.

Still, it wouldn't be easy to run a business alongside her current job. According to her contract, all sidelines were subject to approval. Elin could probably ignore that: surely no one would notice, and anyway, what she did with her free time was her business. What weighed more heavily on her mind was that it was direct competition for Tobias's company, and if that came out, it would be grounds for tossing her out on the street without notice. That also made it hard to advertise: she had to be sure that no one could trace the ads to her. She had already posted a couple using the simplest means, namely, several online platforms. She had done so without using either her own or her company's name, and as a contact address, she had listed an email that bore no relation to her name and that was a Gmail account. The posts had been running for two weeks now, and she had constantly checked that account, but so far not a single inquiry had come through. The whole thing was more of a test flight, and she had no idea if she could actually swing an assignment. For one thing, it was highly competitive work, and it also depended on the type of job. After all, she couldn't just disappear from the office and devote herself to that. As long as she could handle her business in the evenings and on weekends, it would be doable. But why worry if she hadn't yet gotten a single request? What was that saying? Don't trouble your head about problems you don't yet have.

Elin's thoughts turned to the coming weekend. Maja, her partner, was traveling. As a judo and karate instructor, she'd been asked to hold a weekend class in Copenhagen, so Elin found herself alone and without any plans. She had secretly hoped that a job request would come through after all, but nothing had materialized so far. Never mind—she'd come up with another idea.

As the train pulled in to the *Stadshagen* station, Elin grabbed her purse, rose, and pushed her way through to the door.

2

Elin awoke to a pounding head. Damn, that was way too much wine last night. She made a painful effort to sit. Her throat felt parched—why couldn't she stop after two glasses? She desperately needed some aspirin. Still unsteady on her feet, she stood with care and walked to the bathroom. She rummaged around in the medicine chest and immediately took two tablets, drinking directly from the tap. As she straightened back up, she felt dizzy—everything around her was turning. She closed her eyes until the turning stopped.

Now back in the kitchen, Elin made herself an espresso. She was having a hard time thinking straight—filling the metal basket with grounds, pouring water into the receptacle, and placing the stovetop pot on the burner. She walked into the living room, where the empty wine bottle still stood on the table, along with a bag of cheese crisps. Where was her cell phone? And how late was it, anyway? There it was. The time was shortly after 10 a.m. The screen also showed some emails, including one from her new account. The subject line read "Inquiry." Suddenly, Elin was wide awake and instantly clicked on the email. It had actually landed in her inbox the night before, and had Elin not succumbed to the wine, she never would have missed it.

A woman named Helena wanted her help with keeping an eye on her friend. She had included her phone number and asked for a return call. Elin could hear the water boiling in the espresso pot, so she hurried to the kitchen. Ouch, that was a little too fast—she felt ill. She took a deep breath and poured the coffee into a mug. She needed it badly now.

***

Elin marched up the stairs of the underground station and looked around. She needed to make a right, follow *Vasagatan* for a while, and then make another right at the corner of *Kungsgatan.* The cafe should be at the next corner.

Earlier, after downing the strong espresso, Elin had showered, dressed, and then tried out her voice before the mirror. Finally, she had called the prospective client, who suggested an afternoon meeting at the *Vete-Katten*, a cafe Elin had never heard of till now and that she had to google. It was close to *T-Centralen*, the main metro station, so it was easy to reach. Elin's head felt better—at least, it no longer hurt—though she still felt slightly groggy. For lunch, she had eaten some toast. She couldn't manage anything else, but the toast had done her good. The nausea was gone, and now she had only a minor case of heartburn. Maybe she could risk having a piece of cake at the cafe. It still baffled her that she'd let herself go like that. Normally, that wasn't her style at all, though she had to confess that Maja usually held her back from such idiocy. And if Maja had been drinking with her, they would obviously have shared the wine, and Elin would have drunk only half a bottle. But the wine had tasted so good. And besides, she had felt all alone and wasn't considering the consequences. Then there was her frustration over an unrewarding workweek, and in the end she found herself with an empty bottle. She had staggered first to the bathroom and then to bed. How did the saying go? God punishes small sins at once? Yup, today He had struck—right when she'd gotten a chance at landing her first independent assignment.

Elin pulled open the door to the Vete-Katten (the name means "Wheat Cat") and walked up the small flight of steps immediately behind it. The counter for ordering cakes and drinks was located straight ahead. The tables stood to the right and left in the large L-shaped room. Helena had said she would bring a conspicuous red purse, and Elin could only hope that she hadn't placed it under the table, or she would have to walk around the entire place searching for it. No, that had to be it. In a corner to the left on a small table stood a bright-red handbag, and behind it sat a woman whose blonde hair was tied back in a ponytail and who was absorbed in her smartphone.

Elin walked up to her: "Excuse me, are you Helena?"

9

The woman looked up and smiled. "Yes, exactly. And you must be Elin." She offered Elin her hand as she scrutinized her.

Elin hoped that her make-over measures would be enough to hide her hungover state. "Nice to meet you. I'll get myself a quick coffee. Can I bring you anything?"

"No, thanks. I still have some." Sitting before Helena was a half-full cup of coffee and a slice of Budapest roll that she had already begun eating.

Elin turned and walked to the counter. Her gaze drifted across the offerings. Oh my, this was truly tempting. Did she dare order a piece of princess cake? Better not. That much whipped cream and marzipan would be too much for her stomach just yet. Instead, she'd have a *Kanelbulle*. The yeasty dough and light cinnamon filling should do her no harm. She would have a latte as well.

Once she had paid, Elin carried her tray to the table, being careful to keep it balanced. Helena made room by removing her purse and setting her coffee to the side. Elin examined her closely. She was in her late thirties and good-looking, with understated makeup and a stylish outfit that included a white blouse and a light-blue blazer over it. Her jewelry was certainly not of the costume variety: tasteful earrings set with small gemstones, probably diamonds; a gold necklace with a small pendant that matched the earrings; and a wide bracelet, also made of gold. Helena was obviously well off.

"It's terrific that we could meet so soon, and on a Saturday no less," she said, looking at Elin expectantly.

"No problem." Elin took a sip of her coffee. "Should we get right to it, or would you like to know a bit more about me first?" During the phone call that morning, she had already briefly told Helena about her education and her experience with regard to detective work, though she'd neglected to mention her official position at Secure Assist.

"I think I'll get straight to it and tell you what this is all about." Helena had another piece of cake and then started recounting her story. "I'm worried about my boyfriend, Markus. I've grown somewhat suspicious, since for some time now he's been spending a lot of his free time on the road and is apparently not telling me the truth about his activities."

"How do you know he's not telling you the truth?"

"Well, perhaps I'm wrong about that, but there was at least one time when his story wasn't true. He told me he was meeting a friend, but then I saw that same friend at the shopping center. And there was absolutely no trace of Markus."

"And what did Markus have to say about it?"

"I, uh ... didn't dare ask him. I figured that if there were another woman, he would be unlikely to tell me the truth to begin with, and in the future he would be even more careful. So I kept my suspicions to myself and continued to watch."

"And? Were there more inconsistencies?"

"Nothing obvious. I had a hard time verifying anything. He mostly told me that he had to work. But what I noticed was ... Are you familiar with the iPhone app that lets you track your friends' locations?"

Elin nodded.

"We gave each other access through the app some time ago so that we could each see where the other was at any given time. Normally, I rarely used it except, for instance, when I had to wait somewhat longer for him. But after the story with his friend, I started checking more regularly on his whereabouts. During the day, I could always see him, and his locations definitely had to do with his work. But in the evenings, he would disappear from the app. Maybe he lost the connection, but it seems more likely that he changed the app setting to make himself invisible for those periods."

"What kind of work does your boyfriend do?" Elin's brain was about as malleable as frozen playdough—it was a real strain for her to follow along. She was glad to have at least come up with the question.

"He's a real estate broker. That's why he spends a lot of time driving around Stockholm, even though he finds most of his properties in the south."

"And how long does he disappear from the app?"

"That's what I find the strangest of all. In every instance, he was invisible for several hours."

"But you haven't approached him about that, either?"

Helena hesitated, then took another sip of coffee. "No. Just once. I had dinner waiting for him, and he was already over an hour late. I couldn't reach him with my cell phone, and when he showed up on the app again, he was already on his way home, and it was just fifteen minutes before he arrived. When I asked him about it, he acted somewhat annoyed and accused me of being controlling. I denied that, of course, and explained that it was only because of the dinner that I wanted to see if he was in the area. He calmed down a bit after that, but that was reason enough for me to not broach the subject again. On the other hand, his reaction made me even more suspicious."

"But you still received no explanation for his disappearance on the app?"

"Actually, I did. He claimed his battery had died and that he hadn't noticed until he was in the car and had plugged in his phone to charge it. I obviously can't verify that, but when he's on the road for his work, he's supposed to be reachable at all times. That's why I don't fully believe his explanation, since he was invisible for more than two hours."

"I see. And you're guessing there's another woman lurking in the background." Elin looked at Helena, who nodded. "Do you have any additional, concrete signs of that?"

Helena cast her eyes downward. "No, I can't say that I do."

Somehow Elin had the impression that there was more to tell. "Has your boyfriend's behavior at home changed at all?"

"Yes, actually," Helena admitted, hesitating. "He's often irritated, but he says it's because of stress at work."

"How long have you been together?"

"We've known each other four years and have lived together for almost three."

Elin was pondering the best way of framing the next question, but she was still having trouble thinking clearly, so she simply let it spill: "How's your sex life?"

Helena turned red and shifted uneasily back and forth on her chair. This was apparently an uncomfortable topic for her. Elin's assessment had been right.

"To be honest, it's been happening less often. But that's normal—most relationships are like that." Helena was avoiding Elin's gaze. "What bothers me is that it's been a long time since Markus has seemed especially interested in physical contact, if you know what I mean."

"Goodbye kisses and that sort of thing?"

"No, he still does that, even if the initiative comes from me. I'm thinking more of spontaneous hugs and holding hands."

"All right. Got it." Elin leaned back and took the last piece of her cinnamon roll. "How were you picturing this? Should I just tail your boyfriend for a few evenings?"

Helena nodded. "Yes, exactly. I'm giving you our home address and his work address along with a description of his car, including the license plate number. I've already prepared and printed it all for you." She handed Elin a piece of paper with the promised information. "I can also send you an email, if you'd rather have it electronically."

"Yes, great. Then I'll always be able to access it on my smartphone. Is there a specific day when Markus regularly disappears?"

"No, unfortunately not. He may have some preference for Tuesday, but on the whole, it's fairly random—although I do notice it happening at least twice a week."

"Is it only during the workweek, or does he also disappear on the weekend?"

"Both. He works on weekends as well. That's when the most showings take place."

Of course. Elin should have known that. It really wasn't her day, and now the headache also seemed to be coming back for some reason. Probably from having to concentrate on their talk.

The two women then discussed the financial details of the job. That part was easy: Elin suggested a respectable price, and Helena had no objections. She didn't even hesitate to pay a small advance. After that, Helena stood and said goodbye. She promised to inform Elin immediately if she noticed that her friend had gone astray on a particular day or if he let her know ahead of time that he would be late.

Elin decided to remain at the cafe a bit longer. She got a second coffee, reviewed their talk once more in her head, and made a few notes. Somehow she still had the feeling that Helena had not told her everything. She couldn't point to anything specific, but her intuition told her that Helena was hiding something under her hat. Oh well, all she could do was to hope she wasn't missing any crucial information for her assignment. Never mind. She had landed her first job, even in her hungover state. At least, she could be proud of that.

***

On Sunday, Elin felt well again. She no longer had a headache and could also think clearly. After a jog through nearby *Kristineberg* Park, followed by a shower, she was back up to speed. On her run, she had thought of a few more questions she should have asked during her talk with Helena. For instance, she knew absolutely nothing about her client—what kind of work she did and where, etc. She also had no idea what Markus looked like and had completely forgotten to ask for a photo. She really had been far less on the ball than usual.

The issue with the photo was probably solvable, since most real estate offices had a website with employee contact information, which often included photos. Elin did an Internet search on the company and was in luck: Markus Lager was listed on the site, complete with photo, email, and phone number. She wouldn't have to reveal her weaknesses and ask Helena, after all. Markus was good-looking, though not exactly a lady-killer. But photos could be deceptive—it was hard to capture charm.

In any case, Elin could now start planning the surveillance. Every afternoon after work, she would watch for Markus outside the real estate firm and then tail him. She would have to borrow Maja's car for this, but that would surely be no problem. Maja rarely used her car during the week.

3

E lin exited the door of the office building where she worked. She would have to hurry to begin her surveillance on time. She wanted to avoid letting Markus get too large a head start, or she might miss the time of his meeting. Her tracking program was showing that he was already underway and heading south. The day before, Elin had managed to slip a tracking device onto his car, which was harder than she had imagined. His firm's office had an underground garage that required an access code, and at his home, Markus's BMW was parked inside a gated courtyard. That was another matter she had forgotten to mention to Helena. Of course, she still could have asked her client for access to the courtyard, but since Markus was already home on the first surveillance day, that move was no longer logical.

Yesterday, though, on her second day of surveillance, while Markus was showing a residence and his car was parked on the street, Elin was able to attach a tracking device to the vehicle. Following him was now an easy task. It was a good thing the equipment was available at Elin's workplace and that she was in charge of it. That way, no one would notice if she borrowed a sender and laptop.

Maja's car was parked around the corner. Elin had already paid the parking fee for the entire day, which was a bit pricey but worth it, since now she could take off immediately without first having to pick up the car from the house.

The trail kept leading southwards, evidently out of the city. Elin's laptop sat next to her on the passenger seat, and she kept checking it to make sure she was actually following the green dot on the map. So far, she had not seen Markus's car—the distance between them was too great. She hoped that his current venture was not just another professional matter—a home showing or client appointment—because then her tracking would be pointless. Although ... it was possible that Helena was wrong and that her friend was not involved in another relationship. How long should she tail him then? That was yet another thing they had failed to discuss. Elin cursed herself once more for her excessive winebibbing the night before their first meeting. It really had robbed her of her ability to think. Oh well, she would give it two more weeks at most: if the surveillance still proved fruitless, she would meet with Helena again for another talk.

Elin's smartphone beeped. She had a text message, which she checked at the next stoplight. The text was not from Maja, as she'd supposed, but from Helena, who informed her that her dear Markus had just disappeared from the friend-locator app. All right, that sounded promising and might even mean that something of interest could still take place today.

Elin's motivation strengthened. Now it all hung on lessening the distance between them. She had no desire to reach her goal, only to find that Markus had already vanished into some house.

For the next twenty minutes, the road led south and out of Stockholm. Elin had almost caught up with Markus as he turned off County Road 259 to pursue his course on the smaller byways. Now she deliberately kept her distance: she had no desire to be seen. The speed decreased as the roads narrowed. Hardly a house was in sight; instead, fields took turns with forest. Finally, Markus veered into a small community of vacation homes. Elin followed cautiously, stopping before a garage door to see what destination Markus had in mind. In this area, she would not be able to observe him as planned. If he entered a house, she would immediately stand out. Elin watched the green dot on the screen. Markus continued down a small dirt road on the other side of the colony. Elin started to move again. As she neared the road, she began to have doubts. Should she keep on following Markus in the car? It was a single-lane road, with passing likely possible only every three hundred feet. From what she could see on her screen, the road didn't go much farther. There might be a couple of houses at the end, but nothing more. In a car around here, she would blend about as well as a homeless man in a top-tier restaurant. She had better continue on foot. Should she haul her laptop along? No, that was not a good idea. Moving with that unwieldy thing beneath her arm would be far too hard, and at no cost did she want to be seen. Elin parked the car around the next corner and waited for the green dot to arrive at its goal. The road made several loops; then Markus swerved to the right once more and finally stopped after several hundred yards. To make sure that he didn't start driving again, Elin waited another two minutes and then got out. She had donned a baseball cap and equipped herself with a smartphone, binoculars, a digital camera with zoom, a jackknife, and an extendible baton—you just never knew. After following the dirt road for a while and encountering neither cars nor people, Elin came to the place where Markus had turned off. Not a single house could be seen for miles and miles. But it was here that the forest began, and there could easily still be houses that were tucked away from her sight. Elin decided to leave the road and follow a parallel course on foot through the woods. It would take longer and be more strenuous because of the heavy undergrowth, but at least it would serve as a cover if anyone came.

It was only a short while before Elin reached the end of the road. There stood a small cabin, painted dark red with white window frames and bright-red shingles—entirely typical of the kind found all over Sweden. It was probably a summer house or perhaps a rest stop for lumberjacks. All around her, Elin saw firewood piled in heaps. Two cars stood parked outside the cabin: one was Markus's black BMW; the other, a dark-blue Volvo V70. There was no one sitting in either car, nor was there anyone in the yard. Elin remained under cover of the trees as she carefully circled the grounds. She took her binoculars and tried to look in through the windows, but all she could see were some shadowy movements. She had no choice but to wait. It had all the appearance of a tryst—Markus's lover had probably come early and longingly awaited him. It wasn't too hard to guess what they were doing in there. If she could photograph them through the window and catch them *in flagrante delicto*, that would be best. But by no means would she risk being seen. Elin eyed the piles of wood. She decided to take a chance and crept along the back of a stack of wood until she reached the corner of the house. Then she darted along the cabin wall to a window on one side. Everything went smoothly. Not one thing stirred. She listened attentively, but all she could hear was the murmur of voices. Had they turned on the radio or television? Elin slowly straightened up beside the window and peered cautiously into the hut. She could see only a part of the living room, but there she detected two people, though not in the unambiguous position she had hoped to find. Furthermore, they were both men—she was quite sure of that. One of them was sitting at a table in front of a PC. The other—that had to be Markus—was standing behind him and also viewing the monitor. Elin pulled her head back. What did this mean? Was Markus gay, and was this where he and his lover met? But didn't they have anything better to do than play with a PC? Elin looked inside again. Now she was certain that it was Markus with another man. She turned on her digital camera and checked the flash to make sure it was off. Then she held the camera to the window and took a couple of shots. Yes, the photos were all right. Elin examined the small screen to confirm that both men could be clearly seen. That should be good enough. She might even capture them one more time as they left the house. She snuck back to the woodpile and searched for a hiding place among the trees where she had a good view of the cars and the door. Then she took one more quick shot of the Volvo, making sure that the license plate could be easily read from the photo.

It was a long wait, and the woodland populace was no help. From below came the ants, which she had to repeatedly brush off her pants; from above, the mosquitos descended with their shrill hum. Sadly, Elin had neglected to bring mosquito spray. After all, she hadn't counted on the surveillance ending up in the woods. Why couldn't Markus carry on his affair in the city, like a sensible person?

Almost two hours and a ton of mosquito bites later, the door of the house opened. Elin raised her camera and pointed it at the doorway. But what followed left her so speechless that she almost forgot to hit the shutter release. Out came four men, with Markus among them. One by one, they walked down the three steps before the entrance. The last, who was very tall, locked the door behind him. On saying goodbye, they all briefly raised one hand and shouted "*hejdå*," but there was not a single show of affection or other suspicious action. Then they got in their cars, two men in each, and drove off. Elin remained behind, perplexed. What was going on here? Or rather, what was not going on? This bore no resemblance to a relationship. Nor did she have any clue why these men had to meet in the wilderness if the whole thing was totally harmless.

Elin waited another ten minutes to be sure that no one returned. Then she went up to the house and shot some more photos through each of the windows, even though there was nothing worth noting inside. The setup was primitive: a large room with a kitchenette in one corner, a smaller room with a bed, and a simple bathroom. The only oddities were the two desktop computers in the living room—one on the table and the other on a stand by the wall.

On the way back, Elin would ponder what conclusions she should draw from it all. In any case, she had found nothing to confirm Helena's suspicions.

4

It was Saturday again, and once more, the two women were sitting in the Vete-Katten cafe. As before, Helena had been the first to arrive, this time without the red handbag. Otherwise, she was just as trimly dressed as at the first meeting: black blazer, white blouse, beige pants, gold necklace with a ruby-red pendant—again, no costume jewelry here. Elin had already fetched herself a coffee and now sat down.

Helena regarded her earnestly: "You didn't want to tell me anything over the phone. Now I'm very anxious to hear what you have to say."

Elin sensed a slight reproach. "Yes, Helena, I didn't think it would be appropriate to discuss it over the phone. Even if it's not as dramatic as you seem to fear. To get right to the point, I found no evidence that your friend has been seeing another woman or even having a relationship."

Helena visibly relaxed. She leaned back in her chair. "But you could have told me that over the phone."

"Maybe. But I wanted to tell you the whole story in one sitting. Besides, I have a couple of photos you should see." Elin paused and took a breath. "So you know I've been following Markus for the past few days. On Tuesday, you sent me a text that he'd signed out of the app. On Tuesday and also on Thursday, it soon became clear that he was not on the road for his job."

"True. He came home later on Tuesday. On Thursday, he said nothing, but he didn't come home that late."

"Yes, he had driven to the cabin and spent only half an hour there. Which means that he was already back home by 6:30."

Helena leaned forward and asked suspiciously: "You say 'cabin.' Does that mean he was meeting someone after all?"

"That's right. He met with three men on both days. The cabin is south of Stockholm, in a wooded area near Vidja, which is between Flemingsberg and Haninge. The cabin is quite remote, and Markus drove there alone each time. The other men came in their own car. The first day, the three men were already there, and after Markus arrived, they stayed two hours. Here—I took some pictures of the cabin, the men, and their cars."

Elin spread out a series of prints on the table, and Helena examined them in detail. Elin watched her carefully as she did so, but Helena gave no hint of knowing anything about the situation. She had knit her brow, which had formed a small crease above her nose.

"I don't know these men, and the cabin doesn't look familiar to me, either." Helena looked up. "What are they doing in there?"

Elin hesitated. "Well, that part is still unclear to me. If you want, I'd be happy to look into it more closely and find out more. In any case ... as you can see from the third photo, one of them is sitting in front of a PC, and Markus and this man seem to be looking at something on the monitor. From the next pictures, you can see that there are at least two computers in the cabin. I took the pictures after the men had already left. Both were desktop computers, which is why I'm assuming that the four men meet there often and use this equipment on a regular basis. Maybe they're playing computer games or working on some online business idea."

Helena was staring into space. She seemed to be lost in thought.

Elin continued: "At first, I saw only Markus and one other man, which made me wonder whether he was having a relationship with another man." Helena vehemently shook her head, so Elin quickly moved on. "But there was absolutely no sign of that. All I could see was that they were working together on the PC. And it was all very chummy when they said goodbye. You can see from this photo that one of the men rode off with Markus, but I don't think it was the same one who was sitting at the computer with him." Elin pointed at the different photos.

"I can't imagine that Markus would be involved with another man. That's absolutely ridiculous!"

"Yes, fine, that was just the first thing that came to mind." This was apparently an extremely uncomfortable notion for Helena. Maybe her views on homosexuality were somewhat conservative. Elin figured she had better not mention her own lesbian relationship with Maja. "As I said, there was no hint of a romantic relationship."

"All right, so the pictures were all taken on Tuesday, correct?"

"Yes, that's right. On Thursday, I did not follow Markus to the cabin. Instead, I waited for him at the start of the dirt road. Then all four men returned there a half hour later. I also took these two photos at that spot, but all you can see are the two cars. It's hard to make out who's sitting in them, although it looks like Markus took one of the others with him again. But that evening, I didn't follow them any farther."

What Elin did not say was that the Volvo had stopped for a moment and that the two men inside seemed to be looking at her car. Elin had quickly ducked and hoped that none of the four had seen her. Luckily, the men hadn't gotten out but had driven on after a moment of terror for Elin. Elin also refrained from telling Helena about the tracking device that had allowed her to see how Markus had driven straight home afterwards. He had probably dropped the other man off somewhere along the route. On Friday, when Markus's car was briefly parked in front of the real estate office, Elin had succeeded in removing the device again.

"All right, I understand." Helena seemed content. "I mean, my suspicion that he's been seeing another woman has not proven true. That's good enough for me. Whatever he's doing in the cabin with his chums is irrelevant to me. I have no idea why he's made such a big secret out of it, but that's his business. I don't tell him everything, either."

That made no sense to Elin. In Helena's place, she would want to find out what the guy was up to. But for Helena, the simplest approach to that would be to ask Markus directly. To bring a private detective into the game would be overkill. Anyway, Helena had only hired her to expose a potential affair—or to prove her suspicion wrong, which Elin had managed to do.

After that, they settled the rest of the bill for Elin's services and said goodbye. But Elin was not entirely content with the outcome of the case. She still had a strange feeling whenever she thought of the secret meetings in the hut, but what could she do? It was no longer her problem. She had finished her first assignment to her client's satisfaction, and that was the most important thing. At least, she could be happy with that.

5

lin heard the door to the apartment open. Maja had come home. Elin leapt up and ran to the small foyer. She flung her arms around Maja's neck. "*Hej*, it's so great to have you home. I missed you."

Maja kissed her. "I missed you, too, my love." She took off her wet softshell jacket. Today, it had rained practically all day—rare in Stockholm, even if June almost always brought plenty of showers.

"You must be hungry. I made *penne arrabbiata.*"

"Wonderful! That's perfect for this damn awful weather." Maja shook her long, dark hair and walked over to the mirror to comb it. "Hey, did you happen to notice that guy?"

Elin gave her a questioning look. "What guy?"

"Across the street in the entryway next to the supermarket. Earlier, when I arrived at the studio, he was there, too. And I think I also saw him here yesterday in front of the house. Anyway, I have the impression he's watching me."

"Maybe he has a thing for you." Elin giggled. "Can't say I blame him."

Maja grinned. "Yeah, maybe. But when I looked right at him, he immediately turned around, as though

33

I'd caught him at something. But maybe I'm wrong, and it has nothing to do with me. Could just be a coincidence."

Now Elin's instincts had awoken. "Do you think he's still there? Show me!"

She went into the living room, which was on the street side, positioned herself next to the window, and cautiously peered outside. Maja did the same on the other end.

"Yeah, he's still there. Do you see the guy with the brown parka?"

Elin nodded. "Yes, I do. And now he seems to be looking up here. Don't let him see us!"

Maja moved away from the window to the kitchen. "I'm getting some pasta. You can keep scrutinizing him. You're the detective, anyway."

Elin stayed beside the window another few minutes and watched the man. He had his hood on in spite of the fact that the rain couldn't possibly reach him in the entryway. He stood there, apparently waiting for something, yet also looking up at the house again and again. Of course, it was hard to tell which floor and apartment held such interest for him, but it was strange nonetheless.

After supper, Maja wanted to turn on the television, but Elin asked her to wait: "I want to check on this guy one more time. Maybe he's gone by now." Outside, it was already dusk, and Elin was trying to avoid letting her shadow be seen behind the window. The clock read 9 p.m., and the sun would be going down in about an hour. Elin positioned herself beside the window once more and very carefully moved her head forward. Funny, the guy was still standing there. And yes, now he was raising his head again, and it seemed as though he was looking right through their window. Elin didn't like that at all. She would keep an eye on this man. If he was in fact targeting Maja or even both of them, she would be sure to find out.

6

Another day at the office went by with nothing special going on. But Elin was now on fire, and she constantly checked her mail in the hope of finding a new request, but there was nothing. It was enough to drive her insane! She so wanted another assignment, one that would truly challenge her—one that was even more interesting than Helena's. Elin had driven to the cabin a third time and seen the men there, but since nothing new had come of it, she decided she was done with it.

Now back at her apartment, she had changed into something comfortable and eaten a snack. She was standing in the bathroom washing her hands when Maja came home.

"Elin!" Maja was screaming. The door to the apartment slammed shut. Maja's bag made a loud noise as it landed in a corner, and her rapid footsteps could be heard crossing the living room floor. Elin hurriedly dried her hands. This was not at all like Maja, who was usually the image of calm itself. Something must have happened. Elin opened the door to see Maja standing before her, her hands on her hips. Her face was red; her breathing, quick and shallow.

She stared at Elin, furious: "What have you done? Where did you go with my car?"

"Maja, calm down! What happened?"

"I will not calm down! I want to know where you went with my car. Damn it!" Her dark eyes flashed at Elin.

"Fine, no problem. I'll tell you. Come on, let's sit down." Elin stepped toward Maja and tried to take her in her arms, but Maja pushed her away.

"What? I haven't done anything to you. Whatever it is, I didn't do it intentionally. What's going on with the car? Is something broken?" Elin looked at her, distraught. She had never seen Maja like this before. Usually, it was Maja who had to calm Elin, not the other way around. "Come on, let me hold you in my arms. I love you."

That seemed to work. Maja lowered her eyes, and her shoulders dropped. Elin put her arm around her and drew her close. What was going on? Maja was sobbing. She embraced Elin and held her tight. Her shoulders jerked, and she was howling like a hyena. God Almighty, this must really be bad. Maja seldom cried, and never this hard. Elin was getting seriously worried. What had happened here? After all, she had parked the car in the courtyard, and everything had been fine. Unless someone had tried to break in, but that would have happened later. And why did Maja think Elin was to blame? That wasn't like her at all.

Gradually, the sobbing subsided. Elin led Maja into the living room and sat her down on the couch.

Squatting down before her, she looked into her tear-filled eyes.

"Now tell me everything, and if I'm to blame, I'll admit it right away. Promise! And I'll formally apologize. But I honestly have no idea what could be wrong with your car. I borrowed it again the day before yesterday, but then I parked it in the courtyard, as usual. Everything was still fine at that point. I swear!" Elin raised her right hand.

The corner of Maja's mouth twitched briefly into an unsuccessful smile. She dug around in her pants pocket, produced a tissue, and blew her nose. Then she wiped her eyes with the back of her hand. Luckily, she wasn't wearing any makeup, or she would have looked even worse.

"I was attacked," she finally gasped.

"What? Are you hurt?" Elin couldn't believe it. Maja was extremely well trained—she could perform any self-defense move in her sleep. And what did this have to do with the car?

"No. They only threatened me."

"That's lucky." Elin breathed a sigh of relief. At least, Maja was unharmed. "But who threatened you? Now please! Tell me the whole story from the beginning." Elin gave her a penetrating look. "All right, Maja?"

Maja blew her nose once more and leaned back. "Yeah, OK. So I was walking out of the studio on my way to the underground. Since it was still so light out, I took the shortcut through the park. There was no one in sight other than that guy who's been following me for the past few days. He was sitting on a bench in the middle of the park. I was trying to decide whether to turn around. But then I thought, 'This is my chance to find out what this is all about,' and I walked right up to him. He immediately stood up, and it was only then that I noticed he was wearing a mask. I wanted to go back right away, but when I turned around, there were three other guys standing before me, all with masks as well. I tried to escape to the right, but these guys already had a knife at my throat, and they were restraining me on all sides. Then they pulled me off the path and down into the bushes, and one of them whispered that I should keep my trap shut. I was sure they were going to rape me, and I was desperately trying to figure out how to break free. But then one of them—a tall guy, definitely over six feet—said that they just wanted to talk to me. I didn't really believe that, but I waited to see what they would say."

Elin stared at her, spellbound.

"I need something to drink," Maja said.

Elin rose and went to the kitchen. She had an uneasy feeling for some reason. Four guys, of all things, and one of them very tall. That was surely no coincidence. But why?

Elin handed Maja a glass of water. Maja drank eagerly. "And what did they want?" asked Elin.

"They claimed I'd followed them in my car. And that they didn't like having someone sneaking around behind them. This would be their first and final warning. If they saw either me or the car nearby again, our next meeting would proceed without a lot of talking. They said they'd make short shrift of me." Maja had tears in her eyes again, and she let out several sobs. "I had to confirm that I understood. I obviously said yes. After that, one of them hit me in the stomach full force, and I blacked out. When I came to again, the four of them were gone."

"God, how awful! I'm so sorry—I'm sure they were the same guys I was observing. I just don't understand why they reacted so viciously. I've already put the whole thing to rest. Honestly, Maja, I didn't want to pull you in. I'm sure it was me they were after."

"Yeah, that much was clear to me by then. But did you go back to the cabin another time? You only told me about two surveillances. And the men didn't see you at all, did they?"

"Well, yes, they did. The second time, they stopped briefly next to my—I mean, your car. I ducked right away, but they might have written down or photographed the license plate number. I'm sorry— that was my mistake. The first time, I did better and parked around the corner. I'm sure they didn't see the car that time. Then the day before yesterday, I was there again for the third and last time because I just couldn't get the whole business out of my head. I wanted to get through the surveillance quickly, so I drove the car down the dirt road to the fork where it turns off to the cabin. On their way back, they obviously drove by your car, but I was hoping they didn't see it."

Maja sighed. "But they did. Did you find anything out?"

"No, that's why I put the whole thing to rest. The assignment is done. I just wanted to make sure one more time that nothing new had come up. But it was the same game as the other times: working together on their computers, four guys in two cars—nothing more."

Maja was calmer now. Her breathing was steady again. "I'm sorry I lit into you earlier. It's clear that it wasn't your fault. I just needed to vent my frustrations on someone."

"No problem. I probably deserved it, anyway. When I think of how they could have attacked me instead, then I know that I got off lightly with your tirade. But that should be a lesson to me: I'll no longer use your car for detective work. I see now what comes of that. But tell me, can you describe these guys at all?"

Maja shook her head. "No. They all had on black masks, hoodies, jeans, and sneakers. The one who was following me earlier was wearing a brown parka, as usual—otherwise, I'm sure I never would have recognized him. And as I said, one of the other three guys was very tall. Aside from that, I didn't notice anything special."

Elin thought it over. "It fits in any case. I mean, who else could it be? I just don't understand why they would make such a big deal out of it. If all they're doing is playing harmless computer games, they wouldn't have had such a violent reaction. Something about the whole thing stinks—I've had that feeling from the very beginning. Four guys who meet in secret in a secluded place several times a week ... that can't possibly be harmless."

Maja sat up. "You're not really thinking of pursuing this further, are you? To be honest, I've had enough. I can usually put up a good fight, but four men armed with knives—I'd rather not risk that again. And I can tell you: they meant what they said."

Elin raised both hands in defense. "Stop worrying! Under no circumstances do I want anything to happen to you. But it bothers the hell out of me that they could get away with this intimidation act so easily. In my view, our best move would be to bring in the police. They'd definitely find something interesting here—if only I knew what it was."

"Thanks, but I really have no interest in dealing with the police. You know how overworked they are. And since nothing serious happened to me, I can imagine what priority they would give this incident. Also, if these guys ever caught wind that the police were involved, they'd get in their heads to make good on their threat. I really don't need that, thank you very much."

"Yeah, I know. But this situation doesn't exactly feel safe, either. I mean, how do we know that they'll leave us in peace, even if we just lay low? Think about it. You run across one of these guys by chance. You don't even recognize him, but he alerts the others, and there you are again with a knife at your throat."

Maja looked at Elin in horror. "Do you have to be so graphic? I've got chills running down my spine."

"Sorry."

"You're right, though. It's still a risk. Let me see how I cope with it. Ask me again in a few days — maybe I'll change my mind. But please do not do anything without my consent! This thing concerns me now, too. You can't make the decisions on your own."

"All right, Scout's Honor. I'll discuss everything with you beforehand."

Elin could easily understand Maja's point. And she would keep her promise. On the other hand, her detective instincts had been aroused, and she wondered what lay behind this thing. Just what sort of plot were they hatching in that cabin?

Elin rose and walked to the window. She looked down at the entryway to the house on the other side of the street. There was no one there.

"At least, they seem to have called off their surveillance. I don't see anyone there."

"Sounds good. That's something, anyway." Maja made no effort to check Elin's observation but instead went straight to the kitchen. "I need to eat something now. And a glass of wine would also be good. Now that I think about it, more like several glasses."

That was something Elin could fully endorse. Right now, a little normalcy and relaxation were just what they both needed.

7

Elin was sitting in a cafe near her office, waiting for Lars. She had finally made up her mind to call him and set up a personal meeting outside of work. He had agreed, though he'd naturally asked why. Elin had merely mentioned something about a private issue. She trusted Lars. After surviving two assignments together in the past year, they had become a good team.

Elin was seated at a small table in a corner and had already ordered a glass of water. She didn't want any coffee—she was already nervous enough. Several times now, she had gone through various scenarios in her head about how best to explain the situation to Lars. She had decided to simply stick to the truth and tell him everything from the beginning. Lars's reaction to her moonlighting job would then be apparent. In any event, she didn't think he would betray her to Tobias.

The door opened, and Lars entered and looked around the cafe. At his height, he had a good overview. Now he could see Elin waving. He wound his way around the tables and walked over to her, his left leg dragging slightly, as usual—the result of a gunshot wound during his time with the police.

"Hej, Elin."

"Hi, Lars. Thanks for coming."

Lars took a seat and motioned to the waitress, who immediately came and took his order for a cup of coffee.

"So you've got me in suspense. What's on your mind?"

Elin cleared her throat and lowered her eyes. "Yeah, this is a little awkward for me. I hope I can count on your discretion." She looked him in the face.

Lars eyed her with a combination of surprise and amusement. "You know I can keep my mouth shut. So let's hear it. What's this about?"

Elin took a deep breath. "You already know my problem—I mean, that I'm pretty bored at the office, right?"

Lars nodded.

"That's why I've kept my ears open for private jobs."

Lars raised his eyebrows.

Elin told him the whole story: about her company, the ad, the assignment, and how things had gone from there. Lars listened patiently, without interrupting. His angular face betrayed no emotion and gave no hint of what he thought of her actions. Elin took a break only once, when the waitress came with Lars's coffee.

"So I thought I was done with my first assignment and that I could now concentrate on some new jobs." Elin paused.

"Well, then you wouldn't have needed to tell me the whole story." Lars studied her intently with his steel-blue eyes.

"True, and I probably wouldn't have," Elin had to admit. "But then Maja was first followed and then threatened and even assaulted." She told him about the man in the brown parka—the one Maja and she had noticed—and about the assault in the park.

"Wow, so your first assignment worked out really great." Lars looked at her: "Any suspicions?"

"Of course. It's crystal clear. Those guys noticed the car and tracked Maja down through the license plate number. Now they're assuming that Maja was also spying on them for some reason, which is why they gave her a warning."

"OK. So was there nothing else that struck you during their meetings at the cabin?" He winked.

"No, Lars, there really wasn't." Elin raised her right hand, as though making an oath. "Honest to God. But something's not really legit, or why would they get so worked up?"

"Unless the whole stalking thing had nothing to do with the case. What else can you think of? Any other jobs you haven't told me about?"

"No, that's the only one so far."

"Well, then something in your own or Maja's personal life? A former lover or secret admirer? Or someone whose toes the two of you have stepped on?"

"Lars, I've racked my brains over this. I'm not coming up with anything. You already know that Maja and I have been together for two years. Before that, Maja only saw other women, and I never got serious with any man. Other than that, yeah, we had a bit of an argument with the chick upstairs. But she really doesn't need to hire someone to monitor us, and anyway, she can do that best herself from her apartment."

"What kind of argument?"

"Oh, just little things. First, our music was too loud for her taste. Then she claimed we'd stolen her mail. But there was nothing to it. And frankly, Lars, those guys were talking about 'snooping around' and Maja's car. The only thing that fits is the cabin with the four guys."

Lars took a final sip of his coffee and looked up at the ceiling. Then he turned to Elin. His gaze was intense. "So what are you seeing? How would you like me to help you?"

"Well, first of all, I just wanted to talk to someone about it. And then, there's also the fact that you know what you're doing with this sort of business."

"With this sort sideline, you mean?" Lars grinned.

"No, of course not. Look, Lars, I'm not trying to justify this at all. I just needed to try something new. And I'm completely aware that it's against the rules of my contract. I hope you won't mess things up for me."

Lars shook his head. "Let's just say that I know nothing about the bit with your company, all right?" Elin nodded. She had a look of relief on her face.

"All I know is that they threatened Maja, and of course I'll help you with that."

That made Elin happy. "Oh, that would be so great if you could do that."

"Yeah, of course. You were a huge help to me last year with those two assignments, and you bailed me out of several dangerous situations. So for me to have the chance to return the favor could only be a good thing."

"Thank you, Lars. I really appreciate that about you."

"OK, we've cleared that up. Now what do we do? What information do you have on these guys? Descriptions, license plate numbers, etc.?"

Elin shook her head. "Not much, unfortunately. I obviously have photos of Markus and his three pals as well as the license plate number from his car and also the second car, a Volvo. The guy who was watching us is always wearing his hood, which is why I can't say for sure that he was one of the four men at the cabin."

"Does he still stand in front of your house or stalk Maja?"

"Unfortunately, yes. And that's the only reason Maja has agreed to let me talk to you. If they'd left us in total peace, I think Maja would have preferred to forget the whole thing. Anyway, we saw no one for two days following the assault, but after that, the guy in the brown parka resurfaced. Although he doesn't stand there the whole time anymore—just on and off.

And Maja has seen him outside her studio only once since then."

"All right, well, he's never seen me before. Let me know when the guy shows up again. I'll go there right away, and I won't let him out of my sight. Maybe we'll get lucky and be able to ID him from his address or car. And that way, we'll be able to prove the connection to your assignment. After that, we can talk about what to do next. What do you think?"

"That's exactly what I had in mind."

"Is this guy standing in front of the cafe right now?"

"No, I don't think so. I haven't noticed anyone following me personally. It's always just Maja."

"OK, so he's either outside your apartment or Maja's studio. Will you please give Maja my phone number?"

Elin nodded.

Lars continued: "This evening, I won't be able to make it, because I have to pick up my daughter from soccer practice. But every other evening this week should be no problem."

"Great! Thank you!"

"Like I said, call me as soon as you see the guy standing around near your place. OK, I have to go now." He flagged down the waitress.

"Not to worry, Lars. The coffee's on me, of course."

"Thanks. See you tomorrow."

Lars stood and walked towards the door. Elin followed him with her gaze. Confiding in Lars had felt good to her, though she hadn't expected him to take the bit about her moonlighting business so lightly. He'd already blasted her over other things, but those always revolved around topics that related to his job. This didn't affect him directly, and he even seemed a little sympathetic. In any case, it was great that he was willing to help her.

8

ars was cursing inwardly. The traffic at this time of day was terrible. He had to stop at every light, and in between there was nothing but slow going. Elin had called him a half hour before to report that the man in the brown parka was stationed in front of the house again. Lars had been on his way home at the time and was already almost in Hässelby. He'd briefly considered taking the *tunnelbana*, or Swedish underground, back to town. That certainly would have been faster, but he had no idea if the man in the parka had a car parked nearby. Following him without a car would be hard, and in Stockholm, getting a taxi on the fly was next to impossible. So Lars made up his mind to head back to town in his car, even if it took a bit of time. The guy would surely be standing outside Elin's place for more than twenty minutes.

The traffic was putting Lars's patience to a serious test, but after a good three-quarters of an hour, he finally arrived at Elin's apartment house on Kungsholmen. While briefly stopped at an intersection nearby, he immediately spotted the man in the brown parka standing in the doorway of a house. But finding a parking spot at that time of day was a real problem. Most of the residents were home from work and had already taken the available spaces. Still, Lars was in luck: just now, a car was pulling out two cross streets away, and Lars took the empty space. He quickly paid his parking fee with the EasyPark app on his smartphone. That allowed him to keep his parking options open.

Now back at the intersection, Lars could see that the brown parka was still there—yes, everything was good to go. He scanned the surroundings for a suitable observation post. Positioning himself directly across from the man was not a good idea. It was a perfect place to observe the guy, but the man would also be sure to quickly notice Lars, and that was something Lars wished to avoid. Then he spotted a small patch of green—complete with a bench beside a tree. Perfect. Lars could monitor the guy closely from there, and he would instantly see if he started to move. To get there without going right by the man, Lars switched to the opposite side of the road, passed Elin and Maja's house, and then returned to the other side. The bench was still free, and Lars made himself at home. He sat a little to the side to ensure a good view of the entryway. Then he pulled out a newspaper and began to read. He repeatedly peered over the edge of the paper to check that the man was still there.

The time crawled by. Lars had long since read the paper through and through.

When Lars briefly spoke with his wife Lisa over the phone, Lisa wasn't exactly thrilled that he would be late coming home. Of course, she knew that that was a frequent requirement of his job, but she had been looking forward to spending the evening together. Luckily, they had no special plans, so in the end his wife was OK with it.

Lars had called Elin as soon as he began his surveillance, and all of a sudden, she was standing before him with a sandwich and a bottle of mineral water. That was very nice but also a bit risky. Still, Elin had been cautious and left through a different courtyard entrance to avoid being seen by the lurker.

Now it was almost 9 p.m., and Lars was wondering how long the guy planned on standing around. He appeared to have more patience than Lars, and Lars had had a lot of practice waiting. The more he reflected on it, the stranger the whole thing seemed. And so far, none of it made an iota of sense.

Lars's mind began to wander, and he thought of Midsummer, Sweden's largest and most important festival. In about two weeks, it would be time. Midsummer actually occurred on the longest day of the year, but in pragmatic Sweden, the Midsummer festival took place on a Friday—the Friday closest to the day with the shortest night of the year. At this festival, people all over the country would decorate and set up maypoles. Then everyone would dance around the maypole and sing Midsummer songs. At the family Midsummer buffet that followed, the fun would really begin: the schnapps and beer would flow like water, and for every schnapps, there was a song.

Midsummer was also the day when most of Sweden's children were conceived.

This year, Lars and Lisa had decided to drive to Norrland, where Lars's father was from. His parents still had a summer house there, and this year Lars had reserved it over Midsummer for his family. It would be a long drive, but worth it. There in the north, the celebration was still steeped in tradition—there, where broad daylight reigned for several weeks, for the sun never fully set for two whole months. Lars could already see his two girls before him, each with a garland of flowers in her hair as they danced barefoot around the maypole in their summer dresses. They especially loved the famous "Little Frogs" song. Olivia, Lars's younger daughter, had a genuine knack for it: with every "ribbit" in the song, she would hop around just like a real little frog. Lars had to smile— he was looking forward to it.

Suddenly, Lars looked up. He had detected a movement. And sure enough, something was moving in the doorway: the man in the brown parka was forsaking his post. Lars quickly gathered his things and briskly followed the man, who was heading away from him. The brown parka was not exactly conspicuous, but it was easy to distinguish, so Lars had no trouble keeping the man in his sights. He could still maintain his distance while managing not to lose him. By now, though, there were too few people on the move for Lars to risk getting closer.

They rounded two corners, and the man then headed for the Stadshagen underground stop. He vanished through the entryway and took the escalator down. Lars followed on the adjacent steps. Now arrived at the bottom, he waited on the opposite side of the tracks from the man, but switched as soon as the train pulled in on the other side. He waited for the man to enter one of the cars and then took the one behind it. The train was headed to T-Centralen, where the man in the parka transferred to the southbound green line. Following him was no problem. Lars also had the impression that this fellow was not especially cautious. At least, he never turned around or did a careful survey of his surroundings. The man seemed to feel quite safe and apparently didn't expect to be followed. In the meantime, he had also removed his hood, and Lars was able to see that he had a pronounced receding hairline.

Four stations later at Skanstull, the man got off and exited the underground station. Lars followed. These streets were much more bustling, which meant that Lars could and also had to follow the guy a bit more closely. About ten minutes later, the man arrived at his destination, a multi-story apartment house. Lars took out his smartphone and managed to photograph him from the side immediately before he set foot in the entryway. The man keyed in his code on the access pad beside the door and disappeared into the building. Lars waited another ten minutes or so, but the fellow never reemerged. Which apartment he had entered was something Lars could not establish, so he simply recorded the address on his smartphone and sent it to Elin, along with a picture. Maybe she could find out more through the Internet.

Then Lars set out for home. He hadn't needed his car—but we're all smarter in hindsight. By now, it had grown late. At least, the traffic at that time was no longer an issue, so having his car for the ride home to Hässelby was not so bad, after all. Lars was satisfied with his surveillance, and he hoped that Elin would be, too.

9

Elin was carrying the drink tray into the living room. Lars and Maja looked at her expectantly. She set the tray down and took a seat.

"So let's sum this up. What have we got?" asked Lars.

Elin placed four photographs on the table. She had made a cutout of each of the men and printed them out. "These are the same guys I observed at the cabin."

She took a post-it note and stuck it on the first photo. "This one is Markus Lager, my client Helena Ron's boyfriend. He's 41 years old, works as a real estate agent, and drives a company car—a black BMW 3 Series."

She took another post-it note for the next photo. "This guy always drives the other car, the blue Volvo, which is why I'm assuming the car is registered in his name. If my assumption is correct, his name is Justus Kindell, and he lives in Huddinge. He's 42 years old." Elin had figured this out by sending an SMS request to the department of transportation, *Transportstyrelsen*.

Elin picked up the third photo, which showed the man in the brown parka. "This is the guy who's always standing outside our house. Now, with Lars's photo, we can say for sure that he's one of the four men who were at the cabin. Lars followed him to an address on Söder. Unfortunately, the building has ten apartments, so getting a definite ID is not that easy. How old do you think he is?"

Maja studied the picture carefully. "I'd say also in his early forties. In this picture here, he's not wearing a hood for once. And it's really obvious that his hair is thinning."

"Well, I think with such a pronounced receding hairline, he's probably older. Mid-forties maybe?" Lars threw in.

Elin picked up another printout. It was a list of all the building residents, information that in Sweden was publicly available over the Internet. "If that's true, then that narrows down the choices quite a bit. There are a whole lot of young people living in that building, with their ages ranging from twenty-five to their late thirties. There are also two retired couples and a couple in their fifties. Only two men are in their forties. One of them is forty-three and lives with his forty-year-old wife. The other apparently lives alone and is forty-seven."

"I'm betting on the second," said Maja. Lars nodded in agreement.

"OK, then his name is Kjell Norden." Elin wrote down the name. "I'll put a question mark next to it."

She picked up the last photo. "On the other hand, we know absolutely nothing about this one here. This is the tall, very strong guy that Maja also noticed during the assault."

"They don't exactly look like criminals. They're all normal middle-aged types." Maja was studying the photos in detail.

"Maja," Elin countered, "if you could tell a criminal by his nose, our lives would be a lot easier. And besides, they assaulted you."

Lars leaned forward. "All right, Elin. So we have four men who regularly meet in a cabin south of Stockholm. For three of them, we have a probable ID. We know that they get overly touchy when someone spies on them the way you did, Elin, although Maja was the one who felt it. But we have no evidence that they're doing or planning anything illicit. Maybe they just want to keep their plans a secret, and it's all perfectly legal. Like setting up a new business or some secret society, whether political or whatever."

"Do you find it normal for someone to be standing outside our door all day? And that all four of them should pounce on Maja for the purpose of threatening her?"

"No, I don't find that normal. You're right. It's totally excessive. On the other hand, there are plenty of crazy people who react like that. I'm just thinking of some of the nationalistic movements that aren't especially nice during their demonstrations and definitely not squeamish about dealing with anyone who gets in their way."

"Yeah, or just think of Sweden's far-right party, the *Sverigedemokraterna*." Maja gave Elin a piercing look. "Several of them have committed a whole slew of violent acts. Remember how one of them used a steel pipe on some foreigners in the pedestrian zone? He was even a party leader and a member of parliament."

"Well, all right, but we're not foreigners," Elin countered.

No." Lars replied. "We're just using that as an example of how there's been a major increase in violent behavior in some segments of Sweden's population. That's why we shouldn't be surprised if we also run into that type of person."

"So we should just lie down and take it?" Elin looked at him questioningly.

Lars shrugged. "Yeah, I really don't know how to handle it. But what do you want to do? Confront each one of them to drive home the fact that they've gone too far? That will only lead to further escalation. And then the two of you will be living in constant fear that they'll take the next step. I really don't recommend that."

Maja agreed. "Exactly. Besides, the guy with the brown parka hasn't shown up since the night Lars followed him. Maybe they just wanted to make sure that I obeyed their instructions, and now they're content. I have no desire to stir things up again. Your assignment is over, and if they leave us alone, I'd rather just forget those guys."

"But what if they are in fact hatching some criminal plot or even seeing it through? I have the feeling that something is not quite right."

"Elin, I think there's something you still need to learn. I have full respect for your moral outlook, but as private detectives, we complete our assignments—and that's it. We do not take it upon ourselves to investigate clues on our own in an effort to better the world. That's the police's domain." Lars's expression was stern but benevolent.

"Then should we report it to the police—or what?"

"No way," cried Maja. "That puts us back in the line of fire—especially me. You can count on one hand where the police could get a tip like that."

Lars nodded. "Maja's right. You'd be risking it. Besides, you don't have enough facts for the police to take a real interest. They could maybe drive by the cabin and knock politely on the door, but no prosecuting attorney will issue a search warrant on the basis of what you've got. Besides, you know how desperate the Swedish police are right now. The restructuring has created mass confusion, and the clearance rate is lower than ever. You read about it every day in the paper. So you really can't expect the police to protect you if you insist on staying involved and something happens again. They just don't have the resources for that."

Elin was not at all happy with the outcome of the discussion. "Then we should drive down there one more time and find out more. After that, we can hand it over to the police, and they can turn it into a real case."

Lars shook his head. "Best case scenario, it might work that way. Worst case, those four guys could catch wind of it before the police become actively involved, and they could get really pissed. And let me ask you one more time: as part of which assignment are you conducting this investigation? That is not your job as a private detective. I will also tell you honestly that I won't have anything to do with it. I'm happy to help if these guys keep harassing you, but I will not support any private investigations that are none of your business and that could get us all into trouble."

Reluctantly, Elin admitted defeat. "Yeah, I understand. The two of you are probably right. I shouldn't let myself get mixed up in every little thing. I can't solve every crime that happens to fall across my path."

Maja was visibly relieved. "So let's just shelve it! If none of these guys shows up again, then everything's fine. If they do, then we can talk it over with Lars. Would that be OK with you, Lars?"

Lars nodded. "Of course. It wouldn't be right if these guys continued to watch and stalk you. But I also hope they're happy now and will leave you in peace."

Elin took a sip from her glass. Fine, so this was probably the end of the story. The good part, of course, was that there would be no more ugly situations for Maja. Still, Elin was peeved that she'd no longer have the chance to investigate these guys. She would have loved to stick it to them. But Maja's safety was obviously more important. She couldn't take any chances there: she'd already drawn her into the job far more than she liked.

The three of them clinked their glasses and chatted some more about this and that until Lars finally went home.

10

The attack was unexpected. He had lunged at her from the left, but that was just a bluff, and the hammer fist came suddenly from the right. At the last minute, Maja managed to block the blow but almost lost her balance in the process. Her opponent immediately took advantage and followed with a back kick. Maja went down. She looked up as her opponent bowed respectfully. Damn it! She'd failed to be present for just an instant, and that was all it took.

"Well done, Per. You got me. That's enough for today." Maja stood and bowed in return. Per was one of her best karate students, and there wasn't much more she could teach him. If her concentration lapsed at all, he would even get the upper hand, like today. An hour before, she'd gotten totally off balance as she was coming to the studio and noticed the guy in the brown parka standing out front again. Maja had only spotted him at the last minute, shortly before she opened the door, and it sent chills down her spine. She'd been so glad when he didn't show for an entire week. For the first few days after the talk with Lars, she was still watching for the guy wherever she went, but after that, she truly believed it was over. That was why she was all the more shocked when he suddenly resurfaced today. She simply hadn't expected it.

Maja went into the changing booth and sat down on the bench. She needed to catch her breath for a moment. Did this mean it was starting all over again? She wanted nothing more to do with these guys, to never see them again. The assault in the park had affected her more than she had been willing to admit. That sort of thing just could not happen anymore. A short while ago, when the guy had stared at her, she was able to pull herself together and had merely gone into the studio and opted not to think about it. But by the end of the hour-long session, it had caught up with her and had such a negative impact on her reactions during the match. Now she made up her mind to call Elin, after all. Earlier, she had hesitated, but now it had to be. She opened her locker and took out her smartphone.

Elin answered immediately. "Hi, Maja. What's up?"

"Hi, Elin. Are you busy?"

"No, I'm bored, as usual. What's going on?"

"I really didn't want to tell you, but that guy was standing outside my studio again."

"What? The one in the brown parka?"

"Yeah."

"Where was he standing? What did he do?"

"He was already outside the studio when I arrived, and he was watching me."

"Crap, I really thought this was over and that he wouldn't show his face anymore."

"Yeah, I thought so, too. But now he's scared the heck out of me again. You ... I have to ask you this ... did you do anything else that could have provoked these guys?"

There was brief pause, and Maja could hear Elin clearing her throat.

"Maja, honest to God, I did nothing. We agreed that we wouldn't give them any excuses, and I've stuck to that."

"I noticed that you printed out something from the Internet. That's why I thought ..."

"Yeah, I was trying to find out more about the three guys that we managed to ID. But it was only over the Internet, and I didn't get very far. All I discovered was that the guy in the brown parka is a nurse and that he works at Karolinska Hospital in Huddinge. But there was nothing unusual about any of those three. Which means that there was also no reason for me to get involved. Really, I didn't do anything."

"I believe you. I'm just extremely upset. Why did he crop up again today after a week of peace?"

"Maja, I don't understand it, either. So is he still there?"

"I don't know. I haven't gone back out."

"Go and do it. See if he's still standing there. If he is, I can pick you up after work, and then we can have another talk with Lars."

"OK, will do. Will you hang on?"

"Does a bear shit in the woods? Of course I will."

Maja had to laugh—Elin and her sayings. But Maja had achieved her goal, and she felt a little better already. She emerged from the dressing room, made a slight nod to the receptionist, and walked outside through the entryway. She looked around. No, he was no longer there. He was neither standing where she had seen him earlier nor was he on the other side of the street. She took a breath and raised the phone to her ear.

"Elin, he's gone. I don't see him anywhere."

"Good. Maybe he was there by chance and just wanted to see if you were still around."

"I hope so. Thanks, I feel better. It felt good to talk to you. And I consider it a good sign that he's no longer standing outside the studio."

"Should I come pick you up, anyway?"

"No, don't worry about it. I was making myself needlessly crazy. Let's just forget the whole thing."

"Are you sure?"

"Yes, really. I can handle it. I'm a black belt, after all. I'm going back in to prepare for my next training session."

"All right, see you later."

"Kisses."

Maja was determined to avoid letting Elin take the incident too seriously, only to have the whole situation unravel once more. She could sense that Elin wanted to investigate these men some more, and she didn't want to give her any excuses to do so. It was true that their talk had done her good and the guy was gone. Maja only hoped that he wouldn't pop up again. She'd be sure to watch out for him in the next few days, but maybe this really was the last time she would see his face.

Maja turned and went back to the studio. Now she would resume her training with full concentration. A slip like the earlier one with Per would not be happening again.

11

Elin was back at the cabin. She had found a tree that allowed her to look through one of the windows, and from there she also had a view of the front door and the yard. It was easy to climb the tall spruce with its plentiful branches, even if she'd had to fight her way through a host of needles. Now she was comfortably seated on two neighboring boughs, not to mention well hidden.

When Maja had called that afternoon and relayed that the man in the brown parka had suddenly shown up after more than a week, Elin had reached a conclusion: something unusual must be happening today. Otherwise, the guy would have stayed away. The men had left them alone for quite some time, and in the meantime, neither Elin nor Maja had made any moves in that direction.

But today, something was in the wind—Elin was sure of that. The guy had just wanted to confirm that Maja was hard at work and not snooping around the cabin again. And so, Elin left the office early, rented a car, picked up her gear from home, and drove down there. She had parked the car two corners before the dirt road, left her smartphone and ID inside, and placed the key on the front tire. She did not want to risk having the men identify her and link her to Maja, in case they unexpectedly nabbed her.

Markus's car was already there by the time Elin had snuck through the trees to the hut. The Volvo, however, was not. Inside the cabin, Markus was busy at work, and no one else was in view. Elin had taken out her binoculars and was watching Markus through the window. He had pushed most of the living room furniture to the side to create more space and afterwards set up two large lamps. Now he was mounting a camera on a tripod. Elin's instincts had been right: something was afoot today, and the only question now was "What?" She had to admit that there was nothing overly shady about taking a few shots. Still, she would wait until she knew exactly what was going on. Markus checked the different settings one more time and then sat down at the computer. Unfortunately, Elin couldn't see the monitor—it was facing the wrong way. She zoomed in close with her digicam and took some photos of the room.

For a long time, nothing happened. Markus was still just sitting before the PC. Elin's mind began to wander. One week from today, it would be Midsummer. She had no idea why that came to her just now—maybe because of the flowers on the forest's edge or the tall tree that held her. In any event, she and Maja had made no plans. Not that Elin cared about hopping around the maypole, an occasion to which her parents had always dragged her along. She'd really had enough of that by the time she was twelve at most, even though back then she still half believed the stories people told. And so, she had woven a garland from seven different flowers and laid it under her pillow that night, for it was said you would dream of your future beloved. She didn't, of course—and certainly not of Maja. After that, she'd attended the Midsummer festival only with great reluctance, and once she was old enough to decide for herself, she was done with it. In spite of that, Midsummer was something you clearly had to celebrate. Good food, lots of wine, good company—those were all things she loved. She would broach it with Maja tomorrow. Maybe they could throw a party and invite a few friends.

Just then, Elin remembered that she'd promised Maja she would not make any new moves that had to do with the four guys—definitely not without her consent. Now she was sitting here once again, observing. And she had gone ahead and done so without informing Maja. Still, she knew that if it took too long, Maja would be sure to figure it out. As a precaution, Elin had left a map of the cabin's surroundings in her bedroom at home. It would be no more than a few hours before Maja found the map, assuming she hadn't found it already. Shit, she would be pissed. Yes, Elin had a bad conscience. But what else could she do? She simply had to know what was going on here. If something good came of it, Maja would forgive her.

Now Elin heard the sound of a motor as a car approached. Yes, she had guessed right: the blue Volvo turned into the yard just a few seconds later. She watched as the door of the cabin opened and Markus came out. The other three men got out of the Volvo, and after a quick greeting from Markus, the driver opened the tailgate. The tall man leaned in and pulled out a black bundle, some sort of bag with something heavy stowed inside. Maybe more gear? The man carried the bundle up the short flight of steps that led to the door. Elin looked closely: the bundle appeared to be moving—or was she seeing things? All four men had already disappeared into the cabin. Elin pointed the binoculars at the living room window. The tall man had laid his load on the couch, and the four of them were giving each other a high five. They seemed extremely pleased.

For some time, they all milled about the cabin. Then one man went over to the camera as another turned on the large lights and Markus sat down at the computer. After that, the tall man walked over to the couch and untied the bundle. Elin froze. Damn, this could not be true. Inside the bundle was a little girl, maybe five, six years old. She appeared to be sleeping or unconscious—at least, she didn't move very much. The guy with the tripod and video camera was the same one who always wore the brown parka, and it looked as though he was filming the whole thing. The driver of the Volvo was holding a still camera as he squatted next to the sofa. Now the tall guy began to undress the girl: first, her sandals; then, her little dress; and finally, her underwear, until she lay stark naked on the couch. The tall man stepped to the side to let the other two approach more closely with their cameras. Then they placed the little girl in different positions—some innocent, some obscene—and shot her from all sides. Elin didn't just watch: she hit the camera's shutter release again and again.

Well, if that wasn't enough to interest the police ... except that she'd left her cell phone in the car, so she couldn't alert anyone. What should she do? Run back to the car and call the cops? That was probably her best bet. But what if she missed something crucial? Never mind—she had to get help. At that moment, she saw the girl come to, then squirm and strain to sit. Elin started climbing down the tree. Once down on the ground, she heard a scream that had to have come from the girl. One of the men then roared, and there was applause. After that, all you could hear was a whimpering sound. Bloody hell, what were they doing to her? Elin was seriously torn: run to the car or look in again? The girl shrieked once more. That was it. Elin dashed to the window and looked inside. No, this could not be real. Two of the men were holding the girl while one of them filmed, and the tall guy had pulled down his pants and was standing before the little girl, her legs spread wide. Elin was beside herself—there was no way she could let this happen. But what could she do? She set her camera and binoculars on the ground beneath the window, then removed her baton and pulled it out to its full length. She raced around the corner of the house to the door and cautiously pushed down the handle, which luckily wasn't locked. The girl screamed again. Elin had no real plan: all that could help her now was the element of surprise. Could she knock down one or two of the guys and then grab the girl and run?

Elin stepped into the house and took a deep breath. She found herself in a small, open hallway that led directly to the living room. It was now or never—before these scumbags woke up. With a loud cry, she stormed into the room. Markus was standing before the computer. Elin lunged at him with the baton and struck him on the shoulder and head as he collapsed onto the floor. Only three left, and they all shrank back. Elin leapt onto the couch and threw herself in front of the girl, shielding her.

"Leave her alone, you pigs!" She tried to pull the girl up with her left hand. There was no resistance from the child, but she still seemed very dazed. Hell if Elin knew what those guys had given her.

"Nobody move! The kid and I are going now." Elin raised the baton, ready to strike at any time. Then she stepped away from the couch as she pulled the child behind her. The Volvo driver disappeared to the other side of the room. Good—one less. Meanwhile, the tall guy had pulled his briefs back on and was coming toward her. Elin brandished her baton, and he shrank back. She took another step, then another as she held the two men at bay with her club. Markus still lay on the floor. Elin had just reached the middle of the room when the Volvo driver suddenly reappeared with a large knife in each hand.

"You're not going anywhere, bitch. We're turning things upside down now. Hey, Kjell—catch!" He tossed one of the knives to the man with the balding head, the one who usually wore the brown parka. Kjell caught it, and now Elin was faced with two armed men standing between her and the door. Damn it! Her plan hadn't worked. What should she do? If they captured her, that would be no help to the child. She had to get out of there, and she couldn't do that with the kid in tow.

Elin let go of the girl, brandished the baton one more time to keep the men at bay, and then turned toward the window through which she had watched it all from outside. That window was her only chance. It wasn't too sturdy and had only one basic glass pane. Elin had made up her mind. She made a run for it. The tall guy lunged at her again, but with one blow from her baton, Elin whacked him on the arm and was already past him. She heard him howl—and then she jumped. She curled into a ball, making her body as compact as she could while she flew through the air. With a loud clatter, the window gave way as she tumbled through and landed outside on the grass. She rolled once to cushion the fall, but there wasn't much room, and she crashed into a stack of wood. A stabbing pain shot through her thigh. Elin had no choice—she had to keep going. She raised herself up. God, that hurt! She hobbled to the other side of the pile of wood. Walking was hard—she must have really bashed her leg. Elin hid in the bushes behind the woodpile. There was no way she could run from these guys in this shape. She could also feel an intense pain in her side. Probing around, she carefully pulled out a large sliver of glass. The wound was bleeding heavily.

Just then, Elin heard the men storming out of the cabin.

"Move it! You—to the left. I'll go right. She's disappeared into the woods," one of them yelled.

Elin crouched low to the ground. Two figures appeared, one on each side of the stack of wood. They were the two men armed with knives. They charged into the woods and past her bush. Phew, they hadn't seen her. Now what? Wait? They wouldn't be searching the forest forever, and when they returned, they might look more carefully here. Maybe there was a better hiding place. Or better yet, she could steal her way over to one of the cars. With a little luck, the key would still be inside, and she could take off in spite of her injured thigh. She waited a few more minutes. She still heard the two men, though now they were far away. There was no sound at all from the hut. Elin raised herself up with care. Damn, that hurt. Hopefully nothing was broken. She limped along behind the pile of wood and peeked into the yard. The cars weren't parked too far, the BMW being closest. There was no one in sight, so Elin crept over to the car. She had barely noticed a movement from behind when something hit her on the head—and everything went black.

12

ars was waiting outside the dressing room. His daughter Stina was taking a shower in the clubhouse along with the other girls on her soccer team. She had started playing offense lately; before that, she had always played defense. He had driven her to practice and watched from the edge of the field. In the second half of practice, they had formed four teams and played some short games. Stina had actually scored two goals, and that warmed his fatherly heart. Now he saw her coming with one of her teammates, both with red faces and wet hair, happily chatting together.

Right at that moment, the phone rang. Lars looked at the display—it was a cell phone number. He hit the green button.

"Hello, this is Lars."

"Hej, Lars, it's Maja." Maybe he should save her number, after all.

"Yeah, what can I do for you?"

"Lars, I'm worried about Elin. She's gone, and I can't reach her."

"Do you know where she went?"

"She didn't say anything. I was expecting her to be home by now."

"Well, maybe she went shopping, or she's having a glass of wine somewhere."

"No, I'm afraid she drove back to the cabin where the four guys are."

"Why do you think that?"

"At noon today, the guy in the brown parka was standing outside my studio again. I didn't find that at all amusing, so I called Elin. And now her gear is missing, and on her nightstand she left a piece of paper with a picture of a map that shows the cabin's coordinates."

Lars was hyperventilating. "Oh, crap! Why can't this woman ever stick to an agreement?"

"You know her, Lars. She's probably been gone for several hours, and I just found the paper. I'm afraid for her."

"Did the two of you discuss this beforehand?"

"No, the guys hadn't shown their faces for more than a week. I know, though, that Elin still couldn't get it out of her head. She used the Internet to research the three names we'd found."

"And what was the result?"

"As far as I understood it, there was nothing unusual. Lars, I can't just stay here the whole night and wait for her. What if those guys nabbed her?"

Lars thought it over. He would have to take Stina home, change, and then drive to Maja's. "Maja, I'm at my daughter's soccer practice. Luckily, she just finished. I'll come to your place and pick you up, but I'll need half an hour for sure."

"Thank you, Lars, I'll wait. Hurry!"

"See you soon."

Lars hung up. He would have to make tracks. He turned to his daughter and said, "Hey, Stina. That's great that you made two goals. But now we have to get going and head home fast. Your papa has to take off again, and I'm in a rush. You still got some steam in you, Stina? Let's see who makes it first to the car!"

"Sure, Papa!" And Stina took off. Lars would never catch up, but this way he'd gain a little time.

They arrived at their townhouse a short while later. Lars parked the car in front of the garage but kept the motor running and sprinted into the house. He quickly pulled on his green outdoor clothing and took his backpack and gear, which were always ready to go. Then he bolted for the front door. Lisa blocked his way.

"Are you leaving again?"

"Yeah, Elin is probably in trouble. Her friend Maja and I are going to go look for her."

Lisa knit her brow. "Lars, you're not doing something dangerous again, are you?"

"I hope not."

"Whenever Elin is involved, something happens. And I don't want to be visiting you in the hospital again."

"I know, Lisa. But last year, Elin saved my life. I'm not going to leave her hanging. I'm sure you understand. I'll be careful."

"I hope so. Call me as soon as you can."

"Will do." And with that, he was out the door and running straight to the car.

13

Elin slowly came to. She could hear voices. Her head and her thigh both hurt. She was bound to a chair, and the cable ties were cutting the flesh at her wrists and ankles. The men had stuck a piece of duct tape on her mouth, leaving her only able to breathe through her nose. As she opened her eyes, she could see that she was sitting on a chair in the middle of the living room. The sofa stood across from her, and on it sat the little girl, cowering. Around the girl's neck was a metal band that was secured to the wall by a chain. The girl had pulled her knees close and wrapped her little arms around them. She was whimpering softly. Now, Elin heard footsteps behind her. Someone was coming into the cabin from outside.

"Did you get her?"

"Yeah, Markus whacked her one good." The man with the balding head pointed at Markus, who was standing next to Elin and smacking his left hand with the baton as a show of triumph. Elin recalled that she had dropped the baton as she was hurtling through the window.

"Good job. So where was she?" The speaker was the tall man, who had just come in and was now looking Elin up and down.

"She was sneaking over to my car—back there by the logs."

"So what do we do with her now?" the balding guy asked.

Somebody else came in.

"Look what I found." It was the driver of the Volvo, who was holding Elin's camera and binoculars and now showed them all the pictures she had taken. The small display on her camera jumped from image to image. "She took a ton of photos of us."

Luckily, only that day's images were on the camera. The rest were on a memory card that Elin had left at home.

"That little slut." Markus turned toward Elin. "Why is she even interested in us? Shouldn't we worm that out of her?"

"Not right now. We'll deal with her later," the tall man replied. "First, I want to finish filming the girl. Otherwise, we'll have nothing to show for today."

The others nodded. The tall guy appeared to have the say here.

"Are you still up to it? I mean, after all the crap with this one?" asked the driver of the Volvo.

"Oh, yeah." The tall guy grinned. "Now I'm really in the mood. Could even get a little rougher than usual ..." He let out a raunchy laugh. "There's just one thing I have to do before the fun begins." He turned to Elin. "You, you little piece of shit ... you bashed me with this club earlier, and my arm still hurts. Markus, you already had your revenge. Now give me the stick!"

Markus handed the tall guy the baton. Elin's breathing got quicker. The tall man leaned down and looked her in the eyes. "Enjoy it, you little piece of shit. I promise you, this will be tame compared to what we do to you later."

And with that, he raised his arm and smacked her full force on her right thigh. Elin was in so much agony that she couldn't breathe, and all you could hear through the duct tape was a muffled shriek. The men howled. The blow had struck her on her injured thigh, which must have already been black and blue. It took a while for the pain to subside, so Elin missed the first few sentences of the conversation that followed.

" ... that's why I don't think there's anyone with her. We would have already found him. Does she have a phone?" the tall man was asking just then.

Markus answered: "No, I haven't seen one, and I checked her thoroughly. Even if she does, there's no reception here."

"Good. Then throw her in the next room. Kjell, take the knife along and watch her."

"Uh, Gustaf, can't we just tie her up good and tight? Otherwise, I'll miss the whole session."

"No, we can't risk it. You can leave the door open, but there's no way I want her in that film."

Kjell nodded and grabbed the back of the chair. "Hey, Justus, help me out already."

The driver of the Volvo nodded and hoisted the chair by the front legs. Together, the two men carried Elin into the bedroom and set her against the wall by the bed. Kjell, the guy with the balding head, sat down on the bed and held the knife to her face.

"So ... us two cuties could have a little fun, too, huh?" he whispered to Elin. He grinned at her as he ran the tip of the blade down her throat. Elin shut her eyes. She was bound tight from head to toe and couldn't move at all—she was completely defenseless against this shithead. Elin could feel him sliding the knife across her breast and under her blouse. He pressed a little harder, and the top button fell off. After the third button, he ripped the blouse open, slipped the edge of the blade under Elin's bra where both cups joined, and cut it in two with one jerk. The two halves fell to the side, exposing Elin's breasts.

"Yeah, much nicer, don't you think?" he whispered. His breath stank.

At that moment, the action started back up in the next room. They apparently had everything in place again, and one of them was going at it with the girl. She was screaming "No, no" and wailing. It was awful to hear, but it diverted Elin's tormentor, and he stood and went to the door to devour what was going on in the living room. That was apparently more important than plaguing Elin.

The minutes that followed were horrific. Elin was forced to listen to everything transpiring in the next room, but she could do nothing about it. The men's furious moans and the little girl's wails were interrupted only by terse instructions delivered exclusively by the tall man. Elin could hear "Your turn" and "You, in the mouth—him, below," and she couldn't begin to imagine the details. Just what kind of people were these? Without a shred of compassion? When it was over, all she could hear was the quiet whimpering that came from the girl, and at last the men seemed done.

After that, they reviewed the sequences on the computer and moved the equipment to the side. Markus informed them that he had uploaded everything. Finally, the tall guy said, "Bring in the slut!" And the two men carried Elin back into the sitting room. They set her down with her back to the couch. From behind, she could still hear the girl quietly crying.

"Oh, Kjell, you've already started unwrapping." Markus laughed as the other men howled.

Once they calmed down, the balding guy asked with a devilish look, "Shouldn't we take some pictures of her, too?"

"Kjell, you already know that photos of women that age don't bring in squat. There are lots of much prettier girls who put their photos on the web for free."

"I wasn't talking about the usual naked girl pictures. I was thinking more of a snuff video—you know, we could mix business with the practical end of things and have a little fun on the side." He looked around the circle. "We could strip her down and then each of us take a knife and run the gauntlet. A film that goes all the way to the agonizing end—make a good video, huh? What do you think?"

Elin felt like throwing up. She knew what a snuff video was. It was a series of terrifying scenes that ended with the death of a person. Most of these videos only faked the person's death, but there were some where the whole thing was real, and in certain circles, these videos fetched a lot of cash. Dammit! She'd made a huge mistake. She would never get out of here—they were going to kill her. And she couldn't help the girl, either. It had all been for nothing. Why did she have to do everything on her own? She desperately needed backup, but there was none.

Gustaf, the leader, nodded—to Elin's horror. "Not a bad idea. But not in here. One, it'll make a major mess, and two, it'll go off better in the woods. We'll tie one of her feet to a tree. That way, she can run around a bit without getting away."

The men were thrilled. They were all incredibly excited, like little kids around a Christmas tree. Except that Elin was the present, and she came without any wrapping whatsoever. Elin felt sick to her stomach and was frantically trying to think of what she could do. Maybe she could trick them when they brought her outside the house. As soon as she got rid of this chair, she'd at least have a chance.

Her hopes were dashed to pieces by the next sentence out of the tall man's mouth: "We'll carry her out to whatever tree we pick, chair and all. And we won't cut her loose from the chair until we've strapped her leg to the tree good and tight."

The men murmured in agreement. One of them went to the kitchenette to fetch two more knives.

"Hey, Gustaf, do you want me to give the kid another shot?" Kjell asked. Elin thought back to her web research. The man in the brown parka, whom she had identified as Kjell Norden, was a nurse and naturally knew all about injections.

"Nah, she's not gonna run away. We'll take care of her later. I'm thinking we'll run another sequence with her later on."

"Today?" asked the driver of the Volvo.

"Use your head, Justus! This is already the second time some tramp has been sniffing around here. You think that's a coincidence? We're not safe here anymore, and we need to clear the cabin as fast as we can—by tomorrow at the latest."

"Shit, you're right."

"OK, let's go."

The driver of the Volvo and the balding guy picked up Elin's chair and carried it through the front door, down the steps, and into the forest. Gustaf had already gone ahead and selected a tree. He motioned to the men to walk towards him. A little farther into the forest, and they came to a large beech with enough room around it for what they had in mind. Markus had brought the camera and tripod and positioned them at a suitable distance. Now he was adjusting the settings.

The men set Elin down beside the tree, and Kjell began strapping her leg to the beech with a thick rope.

"I want her naked, like Kjell said," ordered Gustaf.

"It's hard to get her clothes off as long as she's tied to this chair. And if we untie her, there's no way she won't start struggling," replied Justus.

"Then get some scissors," was Gustaf's retort.

Justus turned and ran back to the house, giving Elin another moment of reprieve. What were her options? They wanted her stripped naked and bound to a tree, where they'd attack her with knives. She had only one chance: to get her hands on one of those knives. Then she'd be able to defend herself and also cut herself free of that rope. But she'd have to manage it right at the start. Once they stabbed her, it would all be over. It's just that that psychopath had chosen her left leg as the one to bind with the rope, and her right leg was almost useless, so her mobility was seriously limited. Still, Elin was not about to give up, even if no one with an ounce of sense would have placed their bets on her right now. She closed her eyes. This was not how she had imagined her end.

Justus came out of the house and yelled, "I found some scissors!"

So this was it. Elin took a long, deep breath.

14

ars was driving down the Essingeleden
Expressway, with Stockholm sprawled out to the
left. The *Stadshuset*, which hosted the annual
banquet for the Nobel Prize awards, and the historic
Old Town with its city palace were in clear view
between the stretches of water. Maja was sitting
beside him, her dark hair woven into a braid. She had
also changed her clothes for the drive to the woods.

"Maja, if your assumption is right and Elin is
actually at the cabin, how exactly did she get there?
Did she take your car again?"

"No, it's still parked in the courtyard. That's why I
also thought at first that Elin was taking care of
something else. Until I found the map." The map was
lying in Maja's lap. "She must have gotten a car some
other way."

Lars nodded. Yes, when Elin wanted something,
she always found a solution.

The news came on the radio. The war in Syria, the
refugees in the Mediterranean region, and the poor
popularity rating of the Swedish opposition party
Moderaterna were followed by a local announcement:
a five-year-old girl had gone missing in Tyresö, a
locality southeast of Stockholm. They had found her

bicycle in a nearby wooded area. The organization Missing People was already at the site, and a large police contingent was combing the forest.

This was not good, thought Lars. If Elin really was in danger and they needed police backup, they might have a tough time getting it, since Tyresö was not far from the cabin in Vidja. But Lars would rather not say that to Maja. On the other hand, he still held up hope that Elin might simply be at her observation post and had lost track of the time. In that case, she'd definitely hear about it from Maja.

A quarter hour later, they came to the dirt road.

"Now what? Park here or keep going?" asked Lars.

"Turn the corner here. We can watch at the same time for the car Elin was driving. Then we'll at least know if she's actually here."

"All right, except that we have no idea what kind of car she took."

"Well, there can't be too many cars standing around here."

That was true. The properties were all large, so the owners had plenty of space to park their cars. There was no reason to use the road. Lars turned onto a cross street, but there were no cars there.

"Drive a little further. If you make another left turn up ahead, I think we should end up back on the road we took here."

Lars followed Maja's suggestion. As he made the next turn, they spotted a silver Toyota parked by the side of the road.

"That could be it. Stop here."

Lars stopped the car next to the Toyota, and Maja got out and looked inside. She tried opening the door, but the car was locked. Then she went over to the right front tire, felt around, and did the same thing on the other side. She had a look of triumph on her face as she held up the key. Lars was impressed. Maja pushed the button, and the Toyota unlocked. She opened the door on the driver's side and crawled in. She looked around but found nothing. Then Lars climbed in on the passenger side and opened the glove compartment. There lay a wallet and smartphone, and inside the wallet was an ID.

"This is Elin's. So this is the car she took— probably a rental. And now we also know why we couldn't reach her by phone. But why did she leave it in the car?" Lars asked.

"Probably to be safe, in case someone nabbed her."

"Which hopefully hasn't happened. All right, then let's head to the cabin. We'll leave everything here as we found it—just in case we miss Elin."

"Good idea."

They got out of the car, and Maja locked the Toyota and placed the key on the left front tire. Then they drove back to the beginning of the dirt road, and Lars turned onto it without delay. "Should we drive all the way to the cabin? We wouldn't exactly go unnoticed."

"No, if I remember correctly from what Elin said before, there was another little turnoff. We can park the car there and sneak over to the cabin. I don't want to lose any more time. We need to hurry in case something has happened to her."

"All right. It looks like Elin has also parked here before."

Lars careened around the bends to the fork, where he turned and parked the car by the side of the road, ready to go. He grabbed his backpack and got out.

Maja came over to the other side of the car. "Do you want to take the road or go through the woods?"

"Let's take the road. It's faster, and it will be easier on my leg. If someone comes, we can always hit the bushes."

Maja looked at his leg. "What's wrong with it? Did you sprain it?"

"No, it's an old thing. Gunshot wound in the knee, from when I was with the police."

They set off on their way, moving quickly even if Lars had to make a vigorous effort to drag his leg behind him. They walked in silence, both of them lost in thought. Lars was still hoping to find Elin happily lying somewhere in the underbrush, her camera aimed at the cabin. But she had been gone more than four hours now, and that seemed very long.

Ahead of them stood the cabin, with two cars parked out front. Lars headed to the left between the trees and signaled to Maja to follow. Under cover of the trees, they stole their way past the cars until they came to where they saw the small set of steps that led to the cabin entrance. Lars began to move again, this time around the nearest corner of the house. He scanned the edge of the woods along the hut but could spot nothing. If Elin was lying in wait somewhere, she was well concealed.

The sound of voices suddenly came from the hut, as though some men were watching football and the players had just scored a goal.

"Maja, you're more agile than I am," whispered Lars. "Can you sneak over to the window and look in?"

Maja nodded and slunk away. Lars watched as she stole along the side of the house to the window, raised herself up, and peered inside. She didn't look for long, but hurried back by the same way. Lars watched her anxiously.

Maja had panic in her eyes and gasped: "They have Elin. She's tied to a chair, and the guys have knives."

"Shit. Worst case."

"You can say that again. What do we do now?"

"Call the police." Lars took out his cell phone. "Damn it—no reception. You?"

Maja looked at her cell phone and shook her head.

"Maja, you're faster than me—run back to the car! I think we had a connection there. Then call 112 and tell them that four men have taken a woman hostage and are holding her at knifepoint. Her life is in danger. They need to come now. Got it?"

Maja nodded and was about to take off, but Lars held her back.

"Wait," he whispered. "After that, come right back. We'll meet over there behind the stack of wood.

All right? We may need to step in before the police arrive."

Maja gave him a thumbs up and dashed off.

Lars walked slowly over to the woodpile that he had pointed out to Maja. From there, he had a good overview and would wait for her. He looked at his watch. It was shortly before 9 p.m., though still broad daylight outside. Now, one week before Midsummer, the sun would not be setting for an entire hour, and even then it would never get fully dark. That meant they had to be careful to avoid being caught.

It wasn't long at all before one of the men came out the front door. He was the tallest of them, and now he ran past the cars and into the woods. Lars ducked. Damn it all—had they noticed something? Lars stayed very still, then quietly took his backpack and opened it. As noiselessly as he could, he rummaged around and brought out the pepper spray. In Sweden, it was forbidden to have it for private use, but there was no denying that it was extremely effective. Lars took it with his left hand. Then he unhooked his brass knuckles from his belt and slid them onto the fingers of his right hand. Finally, he removed the knife from his belt, also with his right hand. Now he was armed and ready. If the tall guy happened to sniff him out, he'd be in for a big surprise.

But as the man was returning from the woods, the others emerged and were leaving the cabin. It looked like two of them were carrying something—yes, it was Elin on the chair. It appeared that much of her upper body was bare. The men were all armed with knives, and the tall one shouted that he had found a good tree. What was that supposed to mean? Were they going to hang Elin? Lars braced himself. No way he could let that happen—not for all the world.

There was a noise from behind. Lars turned around, spray in hand. It was Maja. He dropped his hand, relieved. "Did you call?"

Maja nodded. She was out of breath. "The police are coming."

"Listen, Maja, these men have carried Elin into the woods and they're heading to a tree. Every one of them has a knife. I don't know what they're planning, but it doesn't look good. We need to step in. One of them is in the house right now. Can you take him out when he comes out?"

Maja nodded. She pulled out her baton and extended it to its full length.

Lars continued: "Your best bet is to go over there and wait for him by the Volvo. I'll head over to the others, back there by that tree. See them? Follow me there as soon as you've knocked that guy down. Then we'll tackle the other three and get Elin out of there. Agreed?"

Maja nodded and darted over to the Volvo. No sooner was she in position than the first guy came out and yelled into the forest: "I found some scissors!"

Lars rushed off to where the other three were—he would have to move fast. He could hear the fourth guy descending the steps, followed by a thud. For a second, he looked back, but the man was no longer in view. Maja had apparently succeeded.

The next statement by the other men confirmed it: "Hey, Justus, what's up? Did you get too excited and fall down?" shouted one of the men. The other two snickered.

Lars approached them from the side and so far had gone unnoticed. But now there was nowhere to hide. The balding man was holding a rope and standing next to Elin, who was still bound to the chair. Lars recognized him as the one he had followed. The other two, including the tall one, were standing between Lars and Elin. It was time to attack. Lars burst in.

"Hey, who the hell is that?" the man beside Elin bellowed, pointing at Lars. The other two turned, but Lars had already approached the first and decked him with his right fist. The guy fell backwards onto the ground. Lars had no time to deal with him, though: the tall guy was already headed his way. He lunged at Lars with his knife, but Lars yanked out the canister and hit the spray button long and hard.

"Aaah, fuck! What is that stuff?" Writhing in pain, the tall guy dropped his knife as he held both hands to his eyes. Now the balding man was on his way. He'd let go of the rope and was hurtling towards Lars. Where the hell was Maja?

There she was. Maja leapt out and rammed the man in the side. Keeping her balance, she raised the baton, but the balding man had already rolled away and was back on his feet. He quickly checked things out, then turned around and bolted into the woods.

"Come on, we need to free Elin. I'll cut her loose. You keep those guys in check." Lars ran to the chair and sliced the cable ties with his knife. Elin ripped the duct tape from her mouth with her first free hand.

"Thanks! Am I glad you're here. That was close— they were going to finish me off."

Lars was now done with the cable ties. All that was left was the rope around Elin's leg. But it was too thick, and the knots were too tight—it would take too long to undo. Lars handed it to Elin: "You'll have to carry it. Come on, let's get the hell out of here before they're back in business. We'll run to my car."

Elin stood, grimaced, and sat back down on the chair. "Lars, I can't run. My right leg is injured." She looked up at him with a helpless expression.

"I'll carry you," Maja broke in and took two steps toward Elin. "Come on, let's go."

"No, wait! First, we have to go back to the cabin and free the girl," Elin countered.

"What girl?" Lars asked, surprised.

"They're holding a little girl hostage. They've done terrible things to her. Please! We can't leave her behind," Elin pleaded.

Lars thought for a moment. "OK, then we'll all go together. Under no circumstances can we separate. That's the only way we'll have a chance."

Maja laid Elin over her shoulder and walked to the hut, baton still in hand. Lars secured their retreat. The tall man was still kneeling on the grass and rubbing his eyes, while the other lay next to him, motionless. The balding man was nowhere in sight.

Lars, Maja, and Elin made it safely back to the hut, where they saw the fourth man lying next to the BMW. He was moving slightly and seemed to be coming to. Lars aimed the pepper spray at him and waited until Maja and Elin had disappeared into the house. After that, he followed and locked the door. He could bolt it from inside, which he did right away. Then he walked down the hall to the main room and looked around: tall lighting fixtures, a computer, a kitchenette, and a naked little girl huddled on the couch. Behind her, a shattered window. Elin and Maja were sitting next to the girl, who was bleeding from her crotch and still looked totally numb.

Elin had laid her arm around the child and was inspecting the metal collar around her neck. "This is secured by a screw. I need a screwdriver or a knife."

"Here." Lars handed her his knife. "What happened to the window?"

"Oh, that was my attempt to escape," replied Elin.

Just as she managed to remove the screw and open the collar, they heard a noise at the door. Someone was trying to open it from outside. The little girl stared at the hallway in terror.

"Crap, that's what I was afraid of," said Lars. "At least one of them is already back on his feet."

Now someone was pounding against the door with a hard object.

"That door won't last too long. Is there somewhere we can hole up?" Lars was unsure that the sharp glass edges on the shattered window would keep the men out if they failed to break down the door.

"There's a little bedroom back there," Elin answered.

Lars walked over and examined the room. It had a bed, a nightstand, a chair, a wardrobe, and a small window.

"Yeah, let's all go in here. It's better than the big room."

Maja took the little girl in her arms, while Lars went back to Elin and helped her up. Together with Lars, she hobbled her way to the bedroom. Then Lars shut the door, turned the key, and walked over to the wardrobe.

"Maja, help me out. I want to barricade the door with the armoire."

Together, Lars and Maja pushed the armoire in front of the door. Lars assessed the situation: "It won't hold them back forever, but it will buy us some time. At least, we have a better chance of defending ourselves in this room than in the big one."

Elin was sitting on the bed, with the girl beside her. She had wrapped the child in a sheet and laid her arm around her. Lars's knife was lying next to Elin on the other side, and she had just finished using it to free her leg from the rope. The girl was staring blankly into space.

"Now all we can do is hope that the police can make it here fast," said Maja.

"Did you call them? When was that?" asked Elin.

"Right before we rescued you. Although I had to run practically all the way to the car before I got a connection." Maja checked her smartphone. "So the call was twenty-three minutes ago. What do think, Lars, how long before they arrive?"

"We have to figure on half an hour, anyway. And that's only if they have an available unit. Otherwise, it takes even longer. Right now, they have a large contingent in Tyresö, where they're searching for the girl. If we had known that the kid was here, we could have told them that. That would have bumped us to the top of their priority list."

"Can't we call them again?" Elin asked.

"How? There's no reception here," replied Maja.

"There's a telephone over there." Elin pointed at the nightstand. There stood an old-fashioned telephone with a rotary dial.

"Do you think it works?" Maja walked over and picked up the receiver. She raised her forefinger and grinned as they all heard the dial tone.

"They definitely have Internet here, along with everything else they need for those awful pictures of theirs. I'm sure an Internet call would be no problem," Elin explained.

Maja dialed 112. Shortly afterwards, she was on the line.

"Yes, hello, this is Maja Gustafsson. I called close to half an hour ago about an assault on a woman by four men—near Vidja. We just rescued the woman and discovered that the four men were also holding a little girl hostage. We're assuming it's the same girl who's missing in Tyresö. We've barricaded ourselves in the cabin, but the four men are trying to break in right now, and we're in urgent need of help ... yes, I'll wait ... they're on the way? ... OK ... thank you ... yes ... goodbye."

Maja hung up. "The police will be here soon, although I can't say exactly when." She looked at the others. "We're going to make it."

Just then, there was a loud crash followed by a triumphant roar. The men had broken through the front door of the hut. From the next room came the sound of footsteps and voices—there were at least three guys. Lars noticed that the girl began to tremble. Elin held her close, but it didn't seem to help.

"They're in the bedroom," one of the men bellowed from the living room. Lars believed it was the tall one. Someone was working on the latch and then threw himself against the door. The armoire shook.

"Let's go! We can break this door down, too." And they immediately started pounding against the door with something big and hard. The wardrobe shook with every blow, and on the fifth blow, the door made a loud crunch.

Lars looked at the two women. "We'd better get ready. Elin, we're pulling the bed forward. Then you and the kid can take cover in the corner. I want you out of the way."

Elin nodded, took the knife, stood with difficulty, and picked up the child. Maja and Lars pulled the bed forward and set it on its side. Then Elin and the child crept behind it and into the corner. Lars and Maja pushed the bed in front of them and then looked at each other and nodded: they were ready. They got into position, standing side by side in the middle of the room.

The blows against the door were working—there was more and more crunching, and the door had already given way quite a bit. One more hefty blow, and the guys were hooting.

"We've almost got it. One more serious whack."

A short pause. Then the sound of a man lunging against the door. There was a good, loud crash as the wardrobe shook some more. Soon they would be in.

Right at that moment, Elin spoke up: "Do you hear that?"

Lars listened. Oh, yes, that was a good sound—a police car siren. And it seemed to be coming closer. Seldom had he been so happy to hear it.

The men at the door had obviously heard it, too.

"Shit, the pigs. Move it—clear out. Markus, take the PC." There was a commotion outside, and the door slammed shut. Finally, both cars started, and afterwards all was still—except for the sound of the siren, which grew louder and louder. Lars exhaled. That was close.

"Should we go outside?" asked Maja.

Lars shook his head. "We'll wait until the patrol car is here. Don't want to find out that one of those guys is still lurking around here waiting for us."

Maja and Lars set the bed back up, and all four of them sat down on it.

Maja embraced Elin. "Oh, girl, the things you get involved in. Shit, you have no idea how scared I was for you." She stroked her back. "Where are you injured?"

Elin took stock. "My thigh is mush. First, I crashed against a stack of wood after jumping through the window, and then that nutjob slammed it with the baton. I also have a bump on my head, and I'm bleeding here on my side, where a glass sliver went into me."

Maja examined the spots. "You need to see a doctor in any case."

Elin nodded. "Thank you both again for coming. I know I tried to go it alone, against my promise. I'm sorry."

"The main thing is I have you back." Maja hugged Elin once more.

Lars patted Elin on the shoulder. "You have my respect. Your instincts were right again. These guys really are the worst of the worst. I suspect that quite a few people will be thanking you for your initiative. Although it would obviously have been better if we'd done it together."

Elin's green eyes flashed as she gave Lars a frustrated look. "Except that you refused to get involved until I came up with more facts. And I only got those today."

Lars averted his gaze. Yeah, she was right. He probably wouldn't have come if Elin had just asked nicely.

At that moment, a car with a loud siren pulled up outside the house. Lars and the others heard two car doors open. Then a voice shouted: "Police! Drop your weapons and come out of the house with your hands above your heads!"

The cavalry was here. They were saved.

15

Elin had stayed in the bedroom with the little girl. She could hear Lars and Maja explaining the situation to the police. One of the policemen appeared to be a former colleague of Lars's and had recognized him immediately. That made things easier.

Elin could hear Lars speaking: "What we need right now, Tobbe, are two ambulances for my associate Elin and for the little girl that we rescued. They're both sitting back there in the small room. Elin can't walk, and the little girl was abused."

"No problem. My fellow officer is taking care of it. Let's go inside."

From inside the bedroom, they could hear the sound of footsteps coming through the next room. Then a policeman poked his head in as Lars stood behind him. The look on the officer's face was one of horror.

"Ugh, that doesn't look good. Is it serious?"

Elin could imagine the scene: herself—filthy, covered with blood, her blouse torn apart—sitting next to a thoroughly frightened little girl who was wrapped in a sheet with a red stain at its lower end.

"It's all right. I'll survive. I'm more concerned about the girl. She's bleeding very heavily and needs medical attention as soon as possible."

"What did they do to her?"

Elin looked at the child, who appeared to not be following the conversation but just staring listlessly into space. If only Elin knew how to help her.

"They chained her to the wall by her neck and raped her multiple times. I had to listen to it all from in here, and there was nothing I could do. It was horrible." Elin's voice was trembling as she spoke.

"What pigs."

"Did you get them?" asked Lars.

"Two of them—the ones in the BMW—tried to cut across the field and got stuck. The officers in the second police car have already arrested them, and they're on their way to the station. The Volvo got away from us, but the dragnet has been started. We'll get them. On another matter: do we know the girl's name? Is she Ebba, the one who was missing?"

Elin shook her head. "No idea. She won't talk. Maybe her clothes are still in the sitting room, if that helps at all."

"I'll take a look." The policeman went back into the living room, and Elin could hear him rummaging around. She tried once more to speak to the child, but the girl didn't respond to "Ebba," either. She just kept staring into space.

Outside, another car with a siren arrived. There were footsteps, and there appeared to be several people.

"Where is she?" a woman asked. The girl raised her head and looked at the door. Lars stepped to the side to let through a young woman, followed by two policemen and a man in civilian clothing. The woman rushed to the bed and fell down on her knees.

"Ebba, my darling!" The girl said nothing, but only stretched out her arms toward the woman, who held her close. The woman was crying—the tears were streaming down her face.

The two policemen looked at each other, and one of them said: "That's her. I'll pass it on so they can break off the search." The other officer nodded, and they left the room.

The man in civilian clothing had gone over to the woman and child on the bed and was stroking the little girl's head. He, too, was crying. At last, he turned to Elin.

"I'm Anders, Ebba's father. Are you the one who rescued her?"

"Well, yes, but not by myself. My colleague and my friend were also there—and, of course, the police."

"No need for false modesty," Lars broke in from his post by the door. "If Elin hadn't pursued this thing and risked her own life, there would have been no rescue."

The man looked at Elin and took her by the hand. "Thank you so much. I can't tell you how grateful I am to have Ebba back." The woman was still holding Ebba, but she, too, looked at Elin and nodded in agreement. Elin didn't know what to say. She smiled and squeezed Anders's hand.

There was the sound of another siren, and Lars said, "The first ambulance is here."

Elin turned to the man and said, "You go first. I'm not doing as badly. I'll wait for the next one."

"Thank you." The man patted her on the shoulder, and he and his family left the room.

Lars sat down beside Elin. "Feels good, doesn't it?"

Elin nodded.

"Enjoy it—it doesn't happen too often with this job. But your efforts here were also truly extraordinary."

"You think I'll lose my job?"

"Oh, right. If Tobias fires you over this, then he can give me the ax as well." Lars grinned.

The second ambulance pulled up before the house. Now it was Elin's turn: "Will you help me outside?"

"Absolutely. I'd be honored." And Lars propped Elin on his arm as she hobbled off.

Today, they would meet for the third time at the Vete-Katten cafe. Helena had called Elin the day before and asked to have a talk. She had even offered to pay. This time, Elin was there first, and Helena had just sat down. Elin studied her. Helena was always elegantly dressed and meticulously made up, but her makeup couldn't conceal the fact that she wasn't doing well. You could see her bloodshot eyes with dark rings underneath, and smiling was an effort. Helena looked tired and sad.

"Thank you for coming," she began. "These past few weeks have been awful for me. Markus is in custody awaiting trial, and he won't speak to me anymore. The only one he'll see is his lawyer. Our home has been searched by the police, and they've seized a number of things. I've been interrogated multiple times, but they won't give me details. I only know that it has to do with pedophilia, and that's really horrible. That was a genuine shock to me. I mean, I lived with Markus. I loved him. There was even a time when we spoke of marriage. And now this. I really hadn't the slightest suspicion in that direction. My worst fear was another woman—as you know. Yes, the police wanted to know all about the assignment I gave you. One of them even commented that you helped to solve the case. Which surprised me, because nothing you told me could possibly give rise to suspicions of that sort. That's why I wanted to meet with you, in the hope that you could tell me more. As I said to you, Elin, I will even pay you for this." Helena gave Elin a pleading look.

Elin nodded. "Yes, I can tell you a lot. I'm just afraid ... no, I'm sure you won't like it at all."

Helena winced. "That bad?" She swallowed. "Regardless, Elin, please tell me everything. I want to know what happened and what Markus has done. Only then can I decide how to go on from here. And only then can I put my life in order again. Can you understand that?"

"Yes, I can. All right, I'll tell you the whole story. But don't say later that I didn't warn you!"

"Promise."

Elin told Helena about the man in the parka, about how he stalked Maja, and about the assault and threat in the park. Helena stared at her with incredulous eyes. Then Elin told her how she'd gone to the cabin one more time and watched how they had carried in the little girl and stripped her of her clothes. She made no attempt to sugarcoat her description of her risky mission and its consequences. And finally, she told Helena about the rescue by Lars and Maja and also of the police action.

"Incredible ..." Helena shook her head in disbelief. "That Markus and the others should do something so terrible. I can't begin to imagine it. I'm sorry that it put you in such danger. Were your injuries very bad?"

"A couple of scrapes and an injured thigh, which is why I'm still limping. But it will all get better."

"And the little girl?"

Elin looked at her. "The little girl was also rescued."

"Yes, but ... did they harm her?"

Elin hesitated.

"It's all right. You can tell me," Helena insisted.

"At least two of them raped her." Elin finally came out with it.

"Oh my God. That's dreadful. Was ... was Markus one of them?"

"That I don't know. I only heard it—I was in the next room. But he was a part of it in any case." Elin would never forget those minutes. She still had nightmares about it all.

Helena had tears in her eyes and was visibly shaken. "How is the girl doing now?"

"Not well. The family is very grateful to me for the rescue, and I've stayed in contact with them. That's why I have a pretty good idea of how Ebba is doing. Her physical injuries have healed, but there's been enormous psychological damage. She's still not talking, and she's apathetic for the most part. Of course, she's having psychiatric treatment, but the doctors can't say how it will all turn out."

"For God's sake. The poor child. This is all much worse than I feared. I thought it might have to do with child pornography over the Internet, as though that's not already bad enough. But to abduct a child and then rape her ..." Helena covered her face with her hands. Then she wiped her eyes with the back of her hand, smearing her mascara in the process.

"Yes, there were pictures, too," Elin added. "The men did an extensive photo shoot with the girl, and they filmed the whole thing. The plan was to flog the material over several specialized Internet platforms for lots of cash. The police found a whole slew of additional pictures and videos on the men's computers. They also found ties to other groups, so hopefully the police will be able to bust a couple more."

"I see." Helena took out a tissue and blew her nose. She paused and then asked, "What would they have done with the girl afterwards? Let her go again?"

Elin shook her head. "I'm afraid not."

Helena stared at her. "You mean they would have killed the child? Did they say that?"

"No, but the police found a child's corpse buried in the woods behind the cabin. They haven't yet identified the corpse, which has been there for several months."

Helena froze. She looked at Elin in horror. "This is unbelievable. What monsters. And Markus is one of them. It just makes no sense to me. I never imagined he could ever be capable of any of it."

Elin took a sip of her coffee. She decided she'd rather not tell Helena about the snuff video. Helena already had enough to digest.

"So have all four men been caught?"

"Yes. Two of them managed to escape in the other car at first, but the police found and arrested them several hours later. Now they're all sitting in jail."

The two women were silent for a while.

"Helena, can I also ask you something?"

"Yes, sure. What is it?"

"At our first talk, when we were sitting here in the cafe, I got the feeling that you weren't telling me everything. Is there something you've held back?"

Helena raised her left eyebrow and looked out across the room. She appeared to be thinking. "No, not really. I don't know what you mean."

"I asked you about the sexual part of your relationship, and you evaded the question. All you said was that it was happening less often."

"Oh, yes, you're right." Helena gulped. "What I didn't tell you ... yes, well, recently, when we did have it ... for the most part, not much happened. Markus ... he had a hard time ... you know?"

Elin nodded. "He couldn't get it up anymore?"

"Yes," Helena whispered.

"Aha. Right, that fits. I guess he could only have a good time with little girls." Elin noticed the expression on Helena's face. "Sorry."

"It's OK. You're right, unfortunately."

They finished their coffee, and then Helena rose and gave Elin a goodbye hug. She looked utterly defeated. Elin watched as Helena left the cafe. Those four men had truly succeeded in ruining the lives of a lot of people. Elin thought of the little girls and their families, but Helena was also among them, even if she stood the best chance for a new beginning. Elin still wouldn't want to trade places with her.

Elin rose and slowly walked to the exit. Her thigh was still hampering her—it mostly hurt when she had been sitting a while. But she could take her time: today, she had nothing special to do. She would have a cozy evening with Maja, who wouldn't be home for several hours. Maja had forgiven her, though Elin had to faithfully promise to never take such a risk again—and definitely not on her own.

It was a quiet day on the underground, and Elin found a seat right away. The train rolled out of the station, bound for Kungsholmen. Elin looked out the window as it sped through the dark tunnel. She thought once more of Ebba. Next week, she would visit her again, and hopefully Ebba would have made more progress by then. Ebba responded positively to Elin in any case. Last time, a fleeting smile had even passed across her face when Elin arrived. Elin had feared that her presence might trigger dark thoughts in the little girl's mind, but the doctors thought it would be good to have Elin come on a regular basis. Ebba would be living in constant fear, anyway, unable to let go of what happened. And as her savior, Elin represented the light at the end of the tunnel. So twice a week every week, she would go and visit Ebba. There wasn't much Elin could do, but Ebba would let her take her in her arms, and Elin had also begun to read her children's books.

Elin was sure she would never forget her first independent assignment. It hadn't turned out at all the way she had imagined—yes, her work as a detective also had its shadow side. And she would still have to have a serious talk with Tobias, her boss. She was, after all, an official witness at the upcoming trial, where her role in the whole story would unfold in detail. It would be clear to Tobias that she had struck out on her own and accepted an assignment in direct competition to his business. But Lars had promised to stand by her and support her. So either Tobias would fire her, and she would simply continue building her own detective business, or things would change between her and Tobias. Either would be fine with her. The main thing for Elin was the chance to work as a detective. That was the right thing for her—in spite of what had happened. Yes, or maybe even more so after this job.

<u>Statistics on forced sex with children:</u>
A survey of nearly 6000 students at 171 Swedish high schools concluded that 29% of the girls had experienced some form of sexual abuse, with 9% even being subjected to forced sex with penetration. Among boys, the figures were lower: 9.6% and 3%.

* http://www.allmannabarnhuset.se/wp-content/uploads/2015/11/Det-gäller-1-av-5.pdf

Similar figures have been reported in other countries:

* http://www.who.int/mediacentre/factsheets/fs150/en/
* http://victimsofcrime.org/media/reporting-on-child-sexual-abuse/child-sexual-abuse-statistics
* http://www.mikado-studie.de/index.php/sexueller-missbrauch.htm
* https://www.nspcc.org.uk/preventing-abuse/child-abuse-and-neglect/child-sexual-abuse/sexual-abuse-facts-statistics/

Thanks to the reader

I am thrilled that you have chosen my book.

I am even more thrilled that you have read it to the end. I especially hope that you liked it. If so, I would like to ask you for a small favour: take a few moments of your time and rate my book on Amazon.

If you didn't like something about the book, please tell me directly! Your feedback is extremely important to me – this way I get the chance to consider the preferences of my readers.

contact@christertholin.one
www.christertholin.one

My heartfelt thanks
Christer Tholin

About the author

The author is originally from Schleswig-Holstein in   Germany and has lived for many years with his family in Stockholm / Sweden, where he works as an independent management consultant.

He is a great fan of Swedish crime literature and had been planning for a long time to make his own contribution. That has already come to fruition with his first book, "VANISHED?" which is also the first book of the "Stockholm Sleuth Series" introducing Elin and Lars. "SECRETS?" is their second case and "MURDER" their third.

www.christertholin.one

On the following pages you can read a sample from „MURDER?"

MURDER?

Stockholm Sleuth Series, Book 3

By Christer Tholin
2019, Stockholm

Christina's idyllic existence with her husband Patrik comes to an abrupt end when Patrik suddenly vanishes from their suburban home in Stockholm. Christina is precipitated into a hellishly desperate and anguished search for Patrik – which after six weeks turns up nary a trace of him.

At her wits end, she contacts local sleuths Lars and Elin, who, after a brief investigation, reach the conclusion that Patrik simply decided to abandon his cushy existence to embark on a new life – without Christina.

Lars and Elin ultimately trace Patrik's movements to the wooded wilds of northern Sweden, but too late – he's found dead. The police rule his death an accident, but Christina thinks otherwise – and so she asks Lars and Elin to do a thorough investigation of the circumstances surrounding Patrik's demise. Was his death really accidental, or was foul play involved? And was the mysterious Natalia somehow implicated?

Unfortunately, none of the countless leads that Lars and Elin follow up gets them any closer to solving the mystery of Patrik's death. But then they get a startling break that results in Christina having to make a tricky and extremely consequential decision that plunges our three protagonists into a life or death struggle.

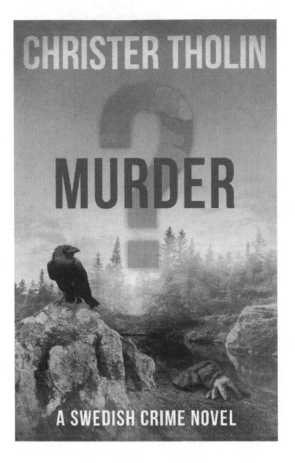

https://www.amazon.com/dp/B07J9HZK23/

PROLOGUE
July 2016

*H*er hand felt so good in his. He was always amazed how soft and delicate her hands were. He was entranced, watching her run along beside him. She was the very picture of loveliness, with her thick blond hair, green eyes and high cheekbones. But this morning he'd had the impression that something was bothering her. She'd disappeared into the bathroom right after breakfast and hadn't been the same since – somehow not as happy and lively as usual. He'd asked her what was going on, but she'd said, "No, nothing, I'm fine."

He was simply crazy about her. He'd never imagined that such a gorgeous young woman could ever be interested in him, much less fall for him. And now here they were beginning a new life together; sometimes he felt like he was dreaming. During the three days since they'd moved into the cabin, the harmony between them had been simply idyllic. And the sex was amazing too – just the love-making he'd been craving, a craving she knew exactly how to slake.

They were approaching the end of the forest path – and the highlight of the walk. The path led to the site of a landslide that had occurred a few years back. The landslide had created a long steep downhill slope that afforded a magnificent view of a large forest meadow dotted with rocks and bushes – and oftentimes animals, which took no notice if you stood there watching them. During a walk they'd taken here a couple of days ago they'd spotted reindeer, which she'd been very excited about as she had never seen a reindeer in the wild.

At the end of the slope they stopped, and he turned toward her. She was staring over the edge of the steep cliff, but she wasn't as radiant today as she'd been during their previous walk.

"Is anything the matter? Did I say something wrong?"

"No, no, nothing like that...I really don't know." She let go of his hand, took a step away from him, and gazed at him. What did the look in her eyes mean? He couldn't tell for sure. He saw a lot of sadness there, but also anxiety. She averted her gaze. What was eating her?

As he was about to again ask her what the matter was, he became aware of a movement behind him. He figured it must be an animal and turned around. A huge muscular man was heading straight for him, causing him to stagger backward. He stepped sideways, into what he realized too late was an abyss. He lost his balance and the last thing he heard was Natalia screaming. His hand clawed the air, as he plummeted downward, almost head first. He managed to grab onto a bush whose thorns dug into his hand; but the bush was too small to break his fall. The branch he'd grabbed broke, and he continued falling.

His last thought before crashing into the ground below was of Natalia.

Made in the USA
Lexington, KY
13 September 2019